The Deed

The Deed

A NOVEL

Tish Mosley

DILYBU Press Nashville, TN

Published by DILYBU Press
P.O. Box 218441
Nashville, TN 37221
www.dilybupress.com

Publisher's Note: This is a work of fiction. Names, characters, places, and incidents are a product of the author's imagination. Locales and public names are sometimes used for atmospheric purposes. Any resemblance to actual people, living or dead, or to businesses, companies, events, institutions, or locales is completely coincidental.

Book Design by Tip Mosley

The Deed/ Tish Mosley. -- 1st ed.
ISBN: 978-0-692-96122-3

For the caregivers

Chapter One

Scots Ridge
Tennessee
January 1946

Rain pounded the tin roof. Slamming like a sledge hammer threatening to wake the baby and his mother. Olive curled her toes around the front door frame bracing herself. She had decisions to make. It was now or never. It was up to her. It always had been. She whispered shameful prayers ignoring what was right and what was wrong. The time for Sunday school thinking had long since passed. Too many choices made in the heat of the moment. Too many years of playing the good sister while watching everything she ever wanted, everyone she ever wanted, going to Beatrix. This time was different. Olive was certain of it. She would see to it.

Standing in the doorway, she watched like so many times before for Tinkum to rise above the hill at the top of the hollow. See him with his slow and easy gate, saunter down the winding road. Hear him whistling a tune. Something he had heard on the radio looping over and over in his mind. That delicious mind of his always churning out some new scheme, some new seduction, some new something that would pull Olive closer to him. As if she could desire him more.

Olive was never one to give compliments and she was even less likely to be impressed with anything anyone did but, she appreciated her daddy giving Tinkum Price a job. She expected him to be attracted to Beatrix. Everyone was attracted to Beatrix. It's just the way of the world. Men and women alike tend to lean in the direction of the beautiful and sweet. Olive knew early enough in life to adjust her thinking and expectations for the leftovers, the scraps, she would glean from others that had enough of Beatrix's weak mind and body. Olive was strong. Strong in ways she had yet to realize.

Grabbing the door frame and leaning out, stretching the length of her long arms, Olive watched as the flood waters rose higher and higher. A water moccasin slithered through the muddy water undisturbed by the pounding rain. The swelling water rushed down the hollow with the sound of a thousand voices. Thunder pealed and lightning split the dove gray sky with its electrifying rip cord that shook the atmosphere from the hand of God.

She prayed one last pleading prayer. The water was rising fast and there was no sign of anyone coming over the hill. "Mud Flats" Olive said with a hiss. The words as filthy as the silt on top of the muddy flood waters. She hated the place.

As if God had heard her complain yet again, the rushing water, a force too fierce to underestimate, pulled at the worn porch and its supports. With a clap of thunder, the porch let go of its grip on the old sharecropper's house with a moan and burst in two as the water claimed it. Olive's knees buckled but she quickly recovered too stubborn to let the flood or Tinkum's absence get the best of her. She was strong. She was sure. Sure of herself, if no one else.

Determined, Olive stayed in the doorway. Muddy water lapping at her bare feet. Forcing its way into the house. Just as she had done for days she watched and waited. Waited for her brother-in-law, Tinkum Price, to return. She needed him. She was ready to admit it. She wanted to give in to the fear but being afraid would be too easy and an unfamiliar luxury compared to what she was facing. She laughed thinking of how many times she had said it was just water under the bridge. Her excuse for doing the things she had done. Never willing to apologize. Now it literally was water that was rushing her to decision. To action. She would worry later. She was too far gone to be second guessing herself and her intentions.

If she lived to be a hundred she would never understand how she could let a man, any man, but especially a man like Tinkum Price convince her to give up any hope of leaving Jessup County for a better life, and instead, pack what few belongings she had and move in with him and Beatrix. Nights spent listening to the newlyweds fueled the resentment and bitterness in her. If it wasn't for the occasional look and touch from Tinkum, she would have ran out of the hollow like her hair was on fire and her tail was catching. Her hopes and dreams to have Tinkum for herself kept her in the one place she vowed she would never be, Mud Flats.

"Ollie?" Beatrix groaned. "Drink. My mouth is so..."

Olive glanced over her shoulder to see her sister fall back to sleep. She made no attempt, great or small, to turn her attention away from the hilltop. Beatrix was left to sink back into the dark oblivion that had become her home. Olive fought the urge to be jealous of Beatrix's means of escape in spite of her failing health. At least, she wasn't standing until her feet ached waiting for a man.

Lightning shot from the sky striking a drowning Sugar Maple in the small front yard severing its limbs. Olive screamed and regretted it immediately when the baby began to cry. Rushing to her sister's bed, she gathered him up into her arms to soothe him back to sleep. Looking at her sister sleeping so deeply she didn't appear to be breathing, Olive kneed the bed just enough to cause Beatrix to gasp but not enough to wake her.

Hearing shouting and the sound of an engine revving, Olive grabbed the bedspread off of Beatrix and wrapped it around her and the baby and rushed back to the opened front door. It had to be Tinkum she told herself. Standing on the ragged edge of where the porch had been, Olive sighed with disappointment to see Ephraim Hatch and Arvis Ange topping the hill in a boat. Ephraim saddled the Jon boat right up next to the house. Its metal shaving the rain soaked boards as the rising water bounced them like fishing bobbers.

"Take hold." Arvis shouted as he reached to take Olive's hand. Her gut reaction was to recoil seeing his fat dirty hand grabbing for hers.

"Easy. That's it. Take it easy. We've got you." Ephraim said in his know-it-all way. The motor idling under his direction. She fought back a snarl thinking of him walking on the water instead of coming to her rescue in his boat.

The boat pitched suddenly. In unison, the threesome turned to see four stiff legs and the nose of Harp Margolus's mule, Lucy, float by with the plow handles cutting channels. They each knew what the other was thinking. Olive swallowed hard pushing down the dread that Ephraim or Arvis would feel the need to say something unnecessary to try to explain it away. As if, being a woman rendered her incapable of understanding the massive consequences of water rising so fast it would pull under a full grown mule still tied to the plow.

No one had time to say two words. In the time it took for their hearts to beat, water poured through the house pushing out everything that was not nailed down. The front door gave way to the rush of water. A flash of white sailed passed its opening. Olive recognized it. It was sheets. Beatrix's bed.

The windows burst pouring water. Ephraim and Arvis and Olive watched stunted as the iron bed slammed against the opened doorway tossing Beatrix out. Their eyes followed her body as it came to a stop floating against an overturned tractor braced on something deep below the water's surface. Her cotton gown ballooned like sails. The iron bed bent and fractured rammed into her. Turning her. Later Olive would remember thinking how peaceful she looked as if still asleep and unaware of what was happening around her. The fast moving current dislodged the backup sending Beatrix down the hollow with the mule, the plow and the iron bed.

Chapter Two

A year earlier...

Gilford Taggart kissed his wife on the check. Patted his son on the head. Reminded him to listen to his mother and boarded the train. He couldn't feel his wife's heart beating beneath her best dress. He couldn't see her hand clutching the two train tickets in her pocket. He couldn't read the worry on her face. Worried that the sweat of her palm would smear the ink causing the man on the train to be unable to read her ticket, hers and the boy's, and refuse to let them board. Gilford Taggart missed all the signs. But, he wasn't a man interested in reading anything but the bottom line.

Across the train station, Tinkum Price sat in the middle of a wooden bench watching people file from one train after another. It reminded him of the hives his Aunt Marly kept. He loved watching her tend the hives. As his eyes watched the train station commotion, his mind saw Marly Price and her slow, graceful body in a cloud of smoke harvesting the honey. A dance among the bees.

Down her body, across the yard, and over to his hand practicing his letters is how his mind traveled the familiar memory. Sometimes a stick would scratch out the letters in the soft dirt at the bottom of the back porch or sometimes his finger. But, always it would begin and end the same way. The alphabet and the few words he had learned to spell with Aunt Marly's help. A for aunt, B for boy. Slow and steady he drew the letters until he got to M. He wanted to remember writing Marly. It would make things easier. If he could. But the memory was always the same. Like a glass of milk that shatters when it falls, splattering sticky and becoming sour, he couldn't change the inevitable. His mind sees his hand with the stick scratch out Mama.

The train horn blasts. The boy pulls his hand from his mother's to cover his ears. He smiles wanting to be brave enough to listen without covering his ears but the horn is too loud and it competes with the engine and the chatter of hundreds of people.

Rosalee Taggart stands as still as a statue. Guarding her every movement praying she isn't drawing attention to her intentions. She watches as her husband of six years fills the window as he takes his seat on the train. His big boned body was the first thing that attracted her to him and will be the last thing she will remember. Silently she begs him to look down at her. Give her one reason not to follow through with her plan. A plan he knows nothing about but still she prays hoping six years of marriage will swell like a wave in this moment and push him to her and not further away. The train horn gives its last blast, the wheels scream, and the bodies in the windows slowly file by without a second glance.

With an hour before the train to Chattanooga would be rolling into the station, Rosalee guided her son to one of the wooden benches in the center of Union Station. Rows and rows of wooden benches with their smattering of couples and individuals anxiously waiting, like wayfaring sinners on church pews at a hellfire and brimstone revival.

"Here George, sit here." Rosalee said. The affection she heard in her voice staved the dread that was bubbling up. She was never overly affectionate but maybe she will be in her new life. George crawled up on the bench and sat too close for Rosalee's comfort to the man sitting alone.

"Not so close George. This man may be waiting for someone and we don't want to be in the way." George looked at the man and scooted an inch or two in the direction of his mother.

"Excuse us." Rosalee said fighting the urge to get up and move to another bench. She had never traveled before and didn't know exactly what to expect but knew she would grow more fearful and nervous if she put too much space between her and the place where the train to Chattanooga would soon be. The closest she ever got to going anywhere was this train station. For six years, she stood and watched George Gilford Taggart board a train and wonder what waited for him at the other end. She waited one year as an unattached girl, one as an engaged bride-to-be and four as the mother of his child.

Tinkum patted the boy on his bare knee. The boy's short pants and scraped knees, his yellowed cotton socks puddled around his tiny ankles dusted with all the places his little scuffed shoes had taken him, reminded Tinkum of a more tender time and the bees and Marly.

"He's fine, ma'am. You both are."

Rosalee smiled nervously, "Well, we just don't want to be in the way."

No matter how hard she tried, she could never escape the feeling of being in the way and she could never stop apologizing for it. Her son felt it too. She could see how it swam in his big blue eyes.

"No. No. Y'all are just fine. There's plenty of room here. Why, I reckon we could sit here 'til this time next Tuesday and not hear a peep out of no one." Tinkum said giving the boy a gentle poke in the ribs causing a ripple of laughter like the sweet sound of water tumbling in a creek.

Rosalee pressed her back to the wooden bench and let the muscles that had been holding her upright give way to the support.

"Where y'all bound? If you don't mind me asking?" Tinkum said keeping his attention on the boy but expecting the answer to come from his mother.

"Chat...ah...Chattanooga." Rosalee said barely above a whisper. Her secret was out. Out of her head. Out of her heart. Out for the whole world to know. Know and judge. But she found no judgment in Tinkum Price.

"Well, that'll be a fun ride, I reckon." Tinkum said still teasing the boy just to the point of correction.

"Where you going?" The boy asked feeling sure of himself and his newfound friend.

"George that's not polite. We don't ask people their business. If they want to share it. They will." Rosalee grew more and more self-conscious and convicted the more she admonished her son because it sounded as if she was admonishing the friendly stranger in a backhanded way.

George drew his knees up close to his chest and hugged them just as a turtle would draw into his shell. Tinkum patted him again on the knee reassuring him that no harm was done. With the warm weight of Tinkum's hand, George stretched one leg and then the other out in front of him becoming distracted watching his shoestrings slowly come untied as he tapped the toes of his brown leather shoes at the edge of the bench.

"Pardon my asking ma'am but is the nature of your visit to Chattanooga unpleasant?" For the first time since she sat down, Tinkum looked Rosalee in the eyes when he spoke to her.

Rosalee's heart clutched in her chest and she feared if she moved the slightest it would crumble and dissolve within her.

"It's just...well, ma'am...it's just I know the look of sorrow in a woman's face. When her tears have long since dried up but the sorrow remains filling every line on her face where once there was laughter." Tinkum spoke as he looked out over the crowd of people. People busy running to or away from something. He wanted to trace the lines on her face with his finger. He wanted to ease her suffering. Hers and every woman he had ever known. It was his Achilles heel.

"I don't mean any disrespect. I'm just a simple man that should mind his own business but something's telling me there's more to your trip to Chattanooga than anyone else holding a ticket."

The silence that fell between them was overwhelming. Tinkum believed he had offended her beyond repair and was ready to take his leave before doing more damage. Rosalee felt if she didn't do something, say something, to make this man understand how desperate for his help she was, she would lose him.

"Groceries. I bought the ticket. The tickets. Two tickets. With my grocery money." Rosalee dropped the words into her lap. Her hands resting in the hollow of her dress. Trembling with two train tickets to freedom sandwiched between them.

Tinkum panned Union Station looking for a man, any man with the look of desperation that matched the brand of desperation on her face. In Tinkum's mind, there had to be a man somewhere wondering where his wife and child had taken off to, and if that man was worth his salt, was searching for them.

Not seeing anyone paying them any particular interest, he began to build his version her of story in his mind. Piecing together a life not worth living any longer, at least not where it began, and needing to make a way somewhere else. He understood that need. Excusing himself from their presence, Tinkum walked across the station floor to the wall of ticket booths. Eyes as big as saucers, Rosalee and her son George, watched as the stranger patiently stood in line for his turn at the window. Just as they were about to remember how to force air in and out of their lungs, Tinkum was making his way back across the vast room smiling at them as the expressions on their faces slowly bloomed matching his.

"The man said the train is running on time. Should be here in the next seven minutes. Gives us just enough time to fetch anything we may be needing before we board."

Rosalee shook her head letting Tinkum know without unnecessary explaining that there was nothing to retrieve. All they had was with them. There would be no baggage.

Standing side by side in the loosely formed line of passengers bound for Chattanooga, Tinkum Price and Rosalee Taggart with her four-year old son, George Gilford Taggart, Jr., watched as the train rolled into the station.

Chapter Three

The rhythmic sway of the train rocked four-year old George to sleep. Curled up like a cat in the sun, the boy's sleep unleashed any inhibitions his mother had about speaking freely. The release came quicker than she had expected. She emptied her heart to a man she had just met. A man she trusted more than her husband.

"But what are you going to do when you get there?" Tinkum pleaded.

Rosalee didn't want to react or to be bruised by his obvious concern but the words landed harder than she appreciated.

"What are you going to do? I'm not the only one operating on assumptions."

Tinkum laughed at her honesty. She was right. Here he was on his way to Chattanooga without a plan one in his craw and just enough money in his pocket to make it to next payday if he still had a job when he got back.

Fletcher Pittman was a fair man but he had already warned Tinkum too many times to count that if he took off again without so much as a word to anyone he was done with him. Tinkum knew the warning carried with it a threat that could and would ruin him for the rest of his life. A fair man is one thing but a shamed man is dangerous.

Tinkum owed Fletcher. And Fletcher was often fond of reminding him of his debt and its increase. Seven years of working for the man had twisted Tinkum up inside. Ram and Arvis and Henry all said he got the better end of the deal when he married Bea. But Beatrix Louise Pittman was not enough to sweeten the sour stomach Tinkum lived with since accepting old man Pittman's offer for work. If anyone, Ram and the boys or Bea or old man Pittman himself knew what and who sent Tinkum searching for his self-respect, there would be more to lose than a couple of dollars at the end of every week. He was banking on the miles of separation to buy him some time. And, he was banking on Bea's twin sister, Ollie to keep her promise.

Laughing Tinkum said, "I reckon you're right. I don't have a plan but if we get to Chattanooga and things don't fall together like we need them to, well, I'll put y'all on whatever train you want to be on and I'll take one back to Nashville. How's that for a plan?"

"Another train?" Rosalee gasped then caught sight of her expression in the reflection of the train window and began laughing. Who was she to pass judgment? Had she not just told Tinkum Price she conjured up the nerve to leave just this morning between cooking breakfast and cleaning up the dishes? What suddenly made her an expert on escaping and starting over?

Remembering the apples she put in her purse just in case she and George got hungry on the way, she offered one to Tinkum. He accepted the apple and suggested she put the other way for later. Taking out his pocket knife and clean handkerchief, he peeled the apple slowly and methodically, letting the long scalloped peel coil onto the white cotton square resting on his knee. Rosalee watched sleepy-eyed knowing the skill it took to not break the peel.

Cutting the apple in half, then into quarters, slicing out the core, and then gently separating it into small slithers, one for her, one for him, Tinkum literally had Rosalee eating out of his hand. Whether he knew it or not, she didn't know. Didn't know and didn't care.

The train ambled along the tracks. The regular rhythm of the wheels on the tracks and the side-to-side sway was intoxicating. The early afternoon sun skipped across fields ready for plowing. Heads rocked on shoulders. Men's heads covered in felt hats with shiny black bands, women's heads with perfumed hair smoothed and tucked into snoods. Rosalee and Tinkum fit right in with no apparent exception. To anyone paying attention, they looked like a family traveling together. A man. His wife. Their child. They could be anyone. Anyone they wanted to be.

The train slowed to a crawl as passengers busied themselves with their departure rituals. The sights and sounds and smells were different. Gone was the quiet hum of the open rail. In its place, the rumbling undercurrent of people. People with places to go.

For the first time since she made up her mind to leave, Rosalee wanted to turn back. What was she thinking leaving everything she knew? She took for granted the security her boring life provided. Here in this moment of suffocating uncertainty, she would trade another day of isolation under that roof he liked to remind her he provided for her, instead of the freedom that was now choking her.

"Step off. Just take them slowly. One step at a time. You'll be fine." Tinkum said as if reading her mind. He held the boy in his arms. George's skinny little arms wrapped around Tinkum's neck. His long black eyelashes batting away the sleep from his beautiful blue eyes. The boy looked like her. That was her one relief. If he looked anything like his father, she couldn't do this. She couldn't look at him day in and day out, a reminder of what she had done, if he looked anything like the man whose name he shared. Light blonde hair, almost white from the sun, stood in sharp contrast to his dark eyebrows and eyelashes. She was teased as a girl for the coloring. It started with her mother. Too jealous of Rosalee and the attention she got, to see the beauty in her own daughter, the woman filled her with shame. Rosalee vowed as a small girl if God allowed her to someday have a child, and if that child shared her coloring, she would never make him or her feel unloved because of it. George didn't know there was anything wrong with having two shades of hair. There was no reason to believe anything other than what his mother told him. He was a handsome boy.

Rosalee slipped her arm around Tinkum's as he maneuvered the crowd. Remembering his offer of putting her and George on another train and him returning to Nashville if things didn't fall together once they got to Chattanooga, Rosalee needed the assurance that Tinkum was not going to walk away or take it upon himself to send her away. At least not until she was ready to part ways, if that was best for them all. Her plan, if she had one, didn't originally include a man but now that she had one, she wasn't going to lose the valuable resource he had become in such a very short amount of time.

"Sport, you stand her with your mother. I'm going to walk over here to check on a thing or two. I'll be right back." Tinkum said patting George on the head and speaking a bit louder than normal conversation.

Rosalee and George watched Tinkum walk away with mixed emotions and blank expressions. Had anyone heard the little announcement and thought anything of it, they would have seen a family of three. A man providing for his family with his firm declaration and a woman and child obeying without rebuttal.

Pushing the change into his watch pocket, Tinkum tucked the newspaper under his arm and handed a small piece of hard rock candy to the boy. Rosalee felt her mouth form the words but nothing, no sound, left her mouth. She would have refused had it been Gilford buying candy and ruining the boy's supper. But then again, she couldn't remember Gilford doing anything of the sort giving her cause to refuse.

"Let's see what we're working with here." Tinkum said unfolding the newspaper. Although they had been sitting since they left Nashville, the small brisk walk to a nearby bench was enough to allow them to stretch their legs and not lose the opportunity to find a place to hatch their plan.

"Looking for the funnies?" George asked. The hard candy rattled against his teeth coating his tongue and lips with a deep cherry red.

"Nope. No funnies. Looking for a room to let." Tinkum said with a wink. Rosalee felt her skin burn as red as the candy coating on her son's lips.

"Hmmm." George nodded as if he knew exactly what Tinkum intended. As if, as men they communicated on a different frequency than Rosalee and all other females.

Folding the paper until it fit in one hand, Tinkum read the advertisement aloud.

"Clean room to let. Quiet neighborhood. No pets. Barters welcomed."

"It doesn't say how much. It doesn't say how big. I mean, is it just the one room?" Rosalee's eyes bounced from Tinkum to George and back to Tinkum again. Both looking back at her with the same flat expression. It will be alright. Their faces seemed to say. Without a word, Tinkum stood. George instinctively put his hand in Tinkum's. And the two walked toward the street with Rosalee following a half a stride behind.

"Excuse me? Could you point us in the direction of," Tinkum held out the folded newspaper to read the street address in the boarding house ad. Before he could get the words out, the man in the tan delivery uniform with "Gus" stitched over its breast pocket, interrupted and said he was on his way to that actual address and offered the threesome to ride along.

Bouncing along on the truck's bench seat, George laughing with each bump in the road as he left his mother's knee, Rosalee could hear the voice of Tinkum in her head reminding her if things didn't fall in place when they got to Chattanooga he would put her and George on another train. It would appear, things were falling right into place. Rosalee stopped holding back and at the next bump laughed with everyone else in the truck cab as George became airborne.

Chapter Four

"**B**ea, if I told you once, I told you a hundred times! I don't know where Tinkum is but if you don't soon find some way to keep your man at home, and out of Pap's crosshairs, you're going to find yourself a widow woman!" Olive shouted into the telephone. She knew someone on the ridge or in Fulton was probably listening. That was the trouble with being on a party line. You never knew who was listening but you always knew someone was. Didn't take swinging a cat to hit one of those busybodies in Fulton sitting on her flat rump listening in on everyone else's business and not taking care of her own. Those women in town were the worse as far as Olive Ann Pittman was concerned. Beatrix Price sobbed on the other end of the connection. Unlike her sister, she worried herself sick about what everyone thought and said behind her back. She did all she knew to do to keep Tinkum at home but trying to keep him in one place was like trying to tie a rope around smoke. It was impossible.

Ram and Arvis and Henry along with Milly and Caroline were forever trying to make excuses for Tinkum. Explaining away his bad behavior on account of how he was raised. As if poor old Marly Price could have done more to root out his wandering before she passed from this world. Beatrix didn't lay blame at the feet of anyone especially another woman, and especially Marly Price. She knew what it was like to love Tinkum. She understood Marly better than she understood herself at times. If it wasn't for Marly and her example, Beatrix felt like she would drift off into the clouds like one of those balloons on a string at the county fair.

Goldie understood. Beatrix knew she did. She didn't have to say more than she did. Everyone else was full of opinion and speculation but Goldie was a woman of action. Without being asked, Goldie had many times gone off on her own looking for Tinkum when no one else would. She found him a time or two and it was Goldie that sent him packing back home. Home to Beatrix.

But this time was different. One sickness after another had taken its toll on Beatrix. She didn't have any fight left in her. Whatever germ was going around was soon to find its way into her weak chest or battered gut. And, if that wasn't enough to keep her from keeping house and an interested husband, her female troubles could bring her to her knees quicker than a sudden fever. Days spent boiling rags and ripping old sheets to make more, had reduced her to someone even she no longer recognized.

She knew. And Tinkum must have known. That nothing was going to take root in a flooded field. That's why she believed he took to the road or the woods or wherever he ran off to when her time came near.

"I just. I just." Beatrix sobbed. Her head hurt passed the point of being able to make sense of what she was trying to say. She held the telephone receiver to her mouth but still nothing came out but more tears.

"What do you want me to do?" Olive asked. Her heart breaking too. Her own brand of guilt and shame kept her hand pressing the telephone receiver to her ear trying to hear what her twin sister was trying to say. Did she know? Was this the call she had dreaded for the last year? Was the love between sisters, twin sisters, enough to bridge the gap of lies?

The line clicked. Olive listened for the sound of her sister's voice. Her sister's crying. Her sister's breathing. But, all she could hear was the buzz and crackle of dead space. If she could crawl into the telephone line and come out on the other end wherever it opened she would take care of business. Whether that business involved comforting Beatrix or flogging whoever it was listening in on the other end, Olive was ready to handle it.

"Come. Here. Please." Beatrix managed before she dropped the receiver onto the cradle. Her emotions had been running high. That was nothing new for her but if she was going to carry the baby to term, she had to follow the doctor's orders. Stay in bed he said. Don't over complicate the matter he said. Let them help he said. She played the speech over and over in her mind. How was this any different than any time before he reasoned with her? She had spent more time in bed from sickness than anyone she knew. Every month. Every full moon. Every chill in the air. Every rolling heat wave. Found her in bed.

Simultaneously, Olive and the unknown eavesdroppers hung up their telephones. Olive raced around her childhood home gathering canned goods, old sheets, and the needlepoint she had been working on to settle her nerves. Waving to Pap walking behind the plow, she stirred up gravel and dust and Pap's curiosity as she pressed the pedal to the floorboard of the '32 Ford Coupe.

On the ridge, Milly Hatch was sitting on her kitchen stool, her nose barely inches from the telephone as she called everyone between Fulton and Tillman that had any interest in what was going on with Tinkum Price and his wife, Bea and her sister, Ollie Pittman.

"He's ran off again..."

"Poor thing. Can't get her feet under her good before..."

"It's the God's honest truth..."

"That Ollie is fit to be tied..."

"Serves them all right..."

"I ain't one to judge but..."

The Ford's brakes grabbed sending Ollie lurching forward against the steering wheel. She rubbed her breastbone and knew she'd have to watch for a bruise. In seconds, she was inside the little house her sister called home.

"Bea! Where are you?" Olive ran in circles in the small house. Two rooms separated by an open doorway covered with a quilt, anyone would be hard pressed not to find what they were looking for with little to nothing obstructing their view.

Out the front door she ran. Around the side of the house. Back around to the front. Once more looking into to the house. Calling out Bea's name. Around the other side of the house. Stopping beside the bedroom window she heard what sounded like a kitten meowing. Turning her ear up. She listened closer. Faint but there, she heard her name. It was Beatrix.

Back inside she stood in the center of the front room listening for the meowing. Listening for her name. Parting the quilt she stood listening. The sun passed by the window filling the room with light. It was there in the sunlight she saw the bed pushed out from the wall. Trapped between the wall and the bed, was her sister.

"Bea! How in the world!" Olive shouted pulling the iron bed out further from the wall. Its feet scratching the dusty floor boards leaving raw lines in their wake.

"You can get yourself in some of the strangest fixes. Don't even bother trying to explain how you could manage to fall between the bed and the wall. I doubt I would understand. Here, are you alright? Did you break anything? Guess you'll be bruised up this time tomorrow." Olive pelted her with words all the while rubbing the tender place on her chest remembering how minutes ago she injured herself beyond explanation. She knew the brakes grabbed but still she forgot and slammed them more times than not. It wouldn't do her or anyone else any good to try to explain why she did the things she did. Just like it wouldn't do anyone any good trying to explain Beatrix.

Chapter Five

Bea's swollen eyelids, heavy with sleep, surrendered leaving Olive alone to find things to keep her occupied. Raising the windows to rid the house of the stale air, Olive's teeth were set on edge to hear the sound of laughter off in the distance. On the other side of the plowed tobacco field with its tender green slips, was the small yellow clapboard house where Ephraim and Milly Hatched lived.

Olive stretched tall to see out the window. She could hear other voices. Her curiosity fueled by her jealousy sent her out the front door and marching across the soft surface of the field sandwiched between the two houses before she had a plan of what to say once she got there.

Standing in the side yard with her husband, Ephraim, and their friends Arvis Ange and Caroline Gentry, Milly Hatch saw Olive cutting across the field long before Olive saw anyone. Birddogs penned in the back corner of the yard turned their noses up to the scent and barked. Olive heard the dogs and her brain ignited.

"Hey y'all wouldn't have happened to have seen Pap's old hound? Thought maybe he made another bee line over here to your dogs." Olive started her story just as she was stepping out of the field and into the side yard. She looked toward the dog pen as if to expect to actually see her father's dog sniffing around it. Allowed to run free because his owner was too proud to keep him penned up, Romeo, a German Short-haired Pointer, had a bad reputation.

"Hey there Ollie! How's Bea? Haven't seen her out lately. She's not sick again is she?" Milly Hatch asked with half-hearted concern but Olive couldn't hear it.

"Bless her heart. I can't remember a time when that poor thing wasn't sick with something." Caroline chimed in needing to be a part of the conversation. Standing too close to Arvis Ange for daylight to pass between them, she tried to appear more concerned than she was matching her strained expression to Milly's. She and Arvis had just gotten engaged and it wouldn't do Caroline to let folks ask her about her ring. She had insisted Arvis drive her around town so that she could show it off to everyone. Milly, too curious to not play along, made a party of it asking their married friends to come over for a chicken supper.

It didn't take Olive long before she saw what was going on and how, whether they were invited or not, it was obvious that Tinkum and Bea would not be joining in on the party and that she was intruding.

Car doors closed behind her as everyone's attention went from her to the couple walking up.

"Ollie, is Bea and Tinkum on their way?" Goldie Filbry asked.

"Folks, how y'all doing?" Henry Filbry said as he came to stand beside his wife.

Shaking her head, Olive didn't bother with answering Goldie with nothing more than a toss of her curls. Goldie knew better than to ask, but she knew she would kick herself later if she didn't bring attention to Tinkum and Bea not being there. She knew just like they all knew, that more than likely Tinkum had found himself too far from home. And, Bea, once again had worried herself sick.

"You say you saw Romeo out here?" Ephraim asked worried about his best birddog, Sadie. Romeo had sired a litter of Sadie's pups last year and Fletcher Pittman still refused to accept responsibility. The last thing Ephraim needed was another litter of Romeo's puppies. He worried the ones he had would roam better than they would hunt.

"Nah, I don't think that was the way she put it, Ram." Arvis said wiping a grin from his tobacco stained mouth. Olive's stomach pitched. She couldn't imagine what Caroline Gentry saw in him. It would take more than the promise of money for Olive to ever lower herself enough to let a man like Arvis Ange touch her much less kiss her. How no one else saw his dirty edges. Edges, she believed would one day take over his entire body, was beyond her comprehension. It served Caroline right. If Olive couldn't wish her sister's poor health on Caroline Gentry, she could at least rest knowing Caroline would be waking up every day for the rest of her life married to a rooting hog.

Just as Ephraim was about to leave the company of his friends to search for the wayward dog, Henry suggested they leave nature to itself and if the dog turned up they'd pack him up and haul him back home. The men laughed at the obvious parallel between Romeo and Tinkum. The joke wasn't lost on Olive and she believed the wives were not as stupid as they acted. It was enough to send Milly inside to tend to her frying pan with her gaggle of girlfriends following behind her. And, enough to send Olive back across the tobacco field with little more than regret for ever coming across it in the first place.

Reaching under the seat of the Ford, Olive pulled out a bag of tobacco and rolled herself a cigarette. She picked the loose tobacco off the tip of her tongue and let the cigarette soothe her nerves. She wasn't about to make a fool of herself, not today, not to that bunch. But, she was wound too tight to go anywhere near Beatrix. And, she wasn't certain what she would do if Tinkum showed up. Part of her wanted to hurt him. Physically hurt him. She knew she could. She also knew she would live the rest of her life regretting it. The other part of her wanted to fold into him. Lose herself in him until she could no longer tell the difference between where he started and she ended. He made her believe it was possible.

The telephone rang its three short rings. That was Tinkum and Bea's ring. Olive ran into the house to grab the telephone. To stop the ringing before it woke Beatrix.

"Pap?" Olive asked.

"How is she?" Fletcher Pittman asked. Suspicious of the telephone as much as he was electricity, always concerned he was going to somehow use it up and not be able to get more, as if that were possible. He rarely burned the one bulb that hung from the ceiling in the center of the front room and rarely did he make telephone calls.

Olive knew it was him when she picked up the phone. She could hear him panting. Most likely his nerves from gathering enough determination to pick up the telephone or from pacing waiting for her to return. Either way, she knew it was him and couldn't stand to see or hear him suffer.

"Pap, she's going to be fine. You know our Bea. But, I'm going to stay on at least for a few days." Olive tried to be gentle and not condescending. Pap may be simple but he wasn't stupid. She also knew better than to say too much or too little to give way to further suspicions about Tinkum.

Fletcher grunted or cleared his throat or some such as what men do when they can't find the words and ended the call. Olive exhaled and dropped the last of the cigarette into a cold cup of day old coffee.

Chapter Six

The moon peeped through the lace curtains spreading curly shadows across the bedroom. Rosalee measured her breathing begging her body to relax and give her a restful night's sleep. But sleep was as far away as the home and husband she had left in Nashville. She pulled the candlewick bedspread up over her son's shoulders. Resting on her side, she gave in to the restlessness and studied the moon.

"Can't sleep?" Tinkum whispered.

"No. How about you?" Rosalee answered worried she would wake her son.

"No." Tinkum said exhaling.

"Is it the bed?" Rosalee asked praying he wouldn't make her feel guilty for sleeping on the bed with her son and leaving him to the trundle below.

Shifting his weight and rolling onto his side Tinkum said, "It's fine. My Aunt Marly had a trundle bed."

"Marly. So that's your family name? Sorry about that. I mean. Sorry for asking like that and sorry for putting you on the spot with the boarding house lady. I guess Mrs. Posey thinks we are a strange bunch after that conversation at the table tonight." Rosalee was doing her best to apologize. She really didn't want to relive the evening but she knew an apology was needed.

Tinkum laughed thinking about it. He knew they should have exchanged names earlier in the day but never did. Leaving the uncomfortableness of offering their names to the owner of the boarding house to play itself out the way it did.

"I'm sure Mrs. Posey sees all sorts through these doors. She probably didn't give two thoughts to how we answered. Something as simple as a name, sometimes goes in one ear and out another. You just never know. Wasn't like she was asking for a life history." He laughed again remembering the uncomfortable exchange.

"Yeah, but really, I know I had to have sounded like a bumbling idiot." Rosalee said her voice cracking with emotion.

Tinkum couldn't tell if she was upset or holding back laughter. Either way, he knew he needed to get out ahead of her worrying because, for better or worse, they had cemented their names together and as far as the owner of the boarding house was concerned, they were a family.

Sitting up on the trundle, the bed springs chirping at the shift in weight, Tinkum looked over the edge of the bed.

"She misunderstood what you were saying. That's all. But seriously, we need to move on from it. We are the Lee family. We are Rosa, Marly and George. That's all. No need to explain anything further."

Tinkum sat on his left hip peering over the edge of the bed. George's mouth gapped open as he slept soundly just inches from the edge of the bed. Sitting and waiting for his words to sink in and for Rosalee to respond, Tinkum watched the boy sleep. It made him feel safe somehow.

Rosalee raised up too. Looking Tinkum in the eyes she nodded. "I agree. The Lee family. Marly, George, and Rosa." Smiling slightly, her eyes heavy with worry, she held the eye contact for a while letting the strength and intent of his words, the gentle and firm expression on his face, set her own resolve. But, she couldn't hold back the "...but?" when it fell from her lips.

Tinkum wanted to reach up to her. He wanted to take her in his arms. He wanted to make her worries go away. It was his natural reaction. One he was trying to control. He knew that pleading tone in a woman's voice. Begging him to set everything right. He had heard it in his wife's voice. He wanted to fix everything for her. Turn back the hands on the clock to a time before they met, when she wasn't grieving over lost babies and misplaced happiness.

Here he was sitting in the darkness with another woman. A woman that needed him. Pleaded with him too. Fix it. Fix me. Give me happiness.

Remembering how Aunt Marly would turn a situation on its head like shuffling a deck of cards, she could take his troubles and turn them inside out. Showing him. Teaching him. Giving him ways to see life from a different perspective. A different outcome. Her way of thinking had become his lifeline.

Sitting up where he could see squarely into Rosalee's face he replayed the events of the night.

"Think about it this way. There we were, the three of us and Gus, just blown in after supper and looking as road-ragged as a body could be. I'm guessing Mrs. Posey did what she always had done and that was to make us feel comfortable. Offer us a meal, which she did. And, a place to rest our heads, which she did. Asking our names was just making conversation and well, partly how she does business, but she ain't going to do business for long if she mettles in folks' business."

Tinkum paused to gauge his words and their intended outcome on Rosalee's face. The lines around her eyes were softening. Her lips were no longer pursed. Her breathing was slowing.

"When she asked you your name, you answered honestly. Just as if you were answering the preacher. You said Rose-ah-lee. Now, I can't account for the hiccup that came between the Rose and Lee part." Tinkum smiled. Rosalee did too remembering. "But, if I were a betting man, I'd say that was on account of the cabbage you were inhaling by the spoonful and the jostled stomach that it was landing on." Rosalee nodded and smiled broader.

"So, you see how she could have heard it. Rosa Lee."

Tinkum paused thinking to himself that he hadn't really given the name situation enough thought. She was worried about the name she gave as being hers. He knew the name he gave wasn't his. It was close enough to memory to remember and familiar enough to know to answer to but he didn't stop to consider she hadn't used her actual name. George didn't react when he heard his mother's name. He had heard it hundreds of times in his short lifetime. Chances are he heard her explain a time or two that it was Rosalee not Rosa Lee. Realizing that there was more to the name misunderstanding, he slowed his thinking. He shuffled his mental cards. He adjusted his approach. She was trying to tell him something. Something he wasn't hearing.

"We are far away from anyone and anything that can make a difference. Like I said, you're Rosa, that's George there, and I'm Marly. We are the Lee family. As of now and going forward, we are the Lee's. No one is going to question that, I'll see to it."

Rosalee smiled a weak but generous smile and reached out to take Tinkum's hand. With a gentle squeeze that passed in the dark as a handshake, she dropped her hand to the edge of the bed and rested her head on the pillow with George.

Tinkum fell asleep staring at her wedding band and remembering the wife he left alone.

***

"Ollie? You asleep?" Beatrix patted her sister on the back. Olive groaned and rolled to her back.

"Not now. What's up?" Olive asked.

"He's not coming back is he?" Beatrix said fighting tears. She knew Olive didn't want to be woke to her crying again over Tinkum leaving and her wondering if and when he would return. She was about as tired of it as anyone. The crying. The wondering. And the leaving.

"I don't know." Olive said. Her tone was more about being woke from a dream - a dream about Tinkum - than it was about her sister crying.

"I'm sorry. I just..." Beatrix sobbed.

Olive, wide awake stared at the ceiling its paint peeling. Just one more reason to be upset with her wayward brother-in-law. She knew she couldn't turn over and look at her sister. If she did. She would burst into tears too. She had more to cry about it. She not only cried for Bea. She cried for herself too. He had ran out on her too. Something Beatrix, she prayed, would never know.

"Bea, we don't know what's going on in that man's head? And, I think we are better off for not knowing. Silly as he is. No telling what we'd find out if we could read his mind. Why can you just imagine it?" Olive tried to sound cheerful. She was speaking to herself as much as she was her sister. Beatrix was listening. She was taking it all to heart. Olive knew that was good. At least one of them would feel better for it.

"I bet we'd make more sense of reading Lucy's mind than Tinkum's." Olive laughed at her own joke. Beatrix giggled too.

"Lucy? The mule?" Beatrix asked still giggling.

"Yeah, I bet we would understand the workings of a mule's mind better than we could that man's." Olive was holding her belly she was laughing so hard. The iron bed rocking. The two sisters laughing together at the expense of the man they loved.

"Oh Olive, you are a mess." Bea said. Her laughter quailed by the realization that they were just releasing the tension and were still just as alone as when they woke.

Olive turned her back to her sister, readying herself to return to her dreams and the man that filled them. "Yeah. I know."

Beatrix Price rolled toward the window across the room. The moon pinned tight to the upper right hand corner of the bare window. Crickets chirped. In the distance a cow bellowed.

Chapter Seven

Milly Hatch cinched her arms across her waist. Bending double she heaved until nothing more would come up. Nothing but her heels lifting off the wet grass with each ripple of nausea. If she was going to spend the next seven months like this, rushing to the edge of the yard to empty her bladder and then her stomach, she doubted she would survive the pregnancy.

Holding onto the clothesline pole, she rested her head on the cold metal and was for the first time thankful she didn't complain when Ephraim insisted on putting in metal poles for the clothesline instead of using wooden supports. The cold surface eased her throbbing head but quickly absorbed her body heat leaving her to roll her head from side to side to find another cool spot.

In the short distance from the side porch off the kitchen, to the back of the yard where the grass was left too tall for the mower, she could hear Della and Ella bickering. She had left them sitting at the kitchen table waiting for their breakfast of grits when the wave of morning sickness washed over her. Della was fond of cheese in her grits and Ella preferred honey. It didn't take Milly too long to know the two had grown tired of waiting for her to return and had taken matters into their own hands.

Della the oldest by fourteen months was forever the boss over her younger sister Ella. Milly worried that Della's strong personality and particular predications would suffocate the soft spirit that made Ella a sweet and loving child. Her stomach still does a flip when the memory of Della ripping a handful of hair from Ella's head when they were toddlers. Milly tried desperately to cover the memory with happier thoughts and cover the gapping bald spot with bonnets. Ephraim refused to correct the girls and wouldn't abide Milly raising a hand to them. It was probably best they had acquired a more relaxed approach to discipline because Milly knows she would have beat Della within an inch of her little life that day she found the plug of matted hair in her hand had it not been for Ephraim's conditioning.

Della danced around the kitchen with her mother's apron draped over her head. Its long gingham sashes trailing behind her.

"Here! You eat this and shut it!" Della demanded as she covered the top of Ella's grits with a blanket of honey. Ella stared at her bowl of grits in shock. Her face red with anger and soaked with tears. Her words forever trapped in her body.

"Shush you baby! Stop your blathering and eat!" Della shouted sending Ella into a silent tantrum. Her face turning purple.

"Ella! Breathe!" Milly pleaded as she came through the screen door. "Della! Sit!"

Della in a huff sat down in her chair across from her whimpering sister. The apron hanging from her neck down the right hand side of her body. Milly gently removed it and placed it back on the hook on the wall beside the sink.

The two girls, too young for school and too old to be left to play on a quilted pallet, scooped cold grits into their mouths and eyeballed each other over the rim of their bowls. They knew the worst that could happen to them was their mother's exasperated threats of not getting to play with their dolls and instead have to help with the dishes or fold clothes from the line. Secretly, they had made the adjustments in their minds to this sort of exchange and looked forward to helping their mother. For them, it was more like play than anything else. And, they, like their mother enjoyed the praise from the man of the house. With his keen eye for detail, he was always quick to point out how he noticed what had gotten done during the day while he was away. Away taking care of man's business, as he put it. Things he said they wouldn't understand.

***

Arvis wrung his hands thinking through what to do. He had heard more than he should and regretted staying on the line. Especially, after he heard Olive accuse whoever it was listening to get off the line and her private conversation and mind their own business. He felt stupid and ashamed for staying on the line. Like a natural born gossip, he was captivated by things that didn't belong to him.

It wasn't the first time he had eavesdropped. He wrecked his brain trying to remember if he ever listened in on one of Olive and Bea's conversations. He did remember listening in one time as Beatrix begged Tinkum to come home.

She had called around until she found him at the Red Stagg Tavern. Nothing do her but that she insist that Red Connors put her husband on the phone. By the sound of it, Red had no choice if he wanted to keep Beatrix from calling her daddy and have him give Tinkum a strong talking to right there in the middle of his establishment. Arvis wasn't sure who he felt sorry for the most, Beatrix for shaming herself by calling around like that, Tinkum for not having the good sense to stay home or at least wait until his wife was good and asleep before traipsing off for a drink, or poor old Red Connors for protecting his beer joint from the likes of Fletcher Pittman dusting the floorboards with Tinkum Price.

This time was different. He had heard her tell Olive she was expecting. Heard her explaining how the doctor had put her to bed if she planned on carrying the baby. Arvis tried his best not to pass judgment on Tinkum. They had been friends since they both were in short britches. Arvis wasn't sure if he wouldn't turn tail and run too as often as Tinkum does if faced with the same life situations. He thanked the good Lord every day for a woman like Caroline Gentry. She was from good stock. Strong and sweet. She would live to be a hundred and Arvis hoped and prayed he would live just as long to appreciate her.

He was chucked full of news and didn't know what to do with it. Beatrix hadn't shared this with anyone except her sister. As best he could make out from their conversation, Tinkum didn't even know. He had run out just before the doctor got to their place. Beatrix hadn't even had time to settle in on the news before having to deal with him taking to the roads and not finding his way back again.

Arvis knew this when Olive came hightailing over to Ram and Milly's. He knew the story about hunting for old Romeo was just her way of spying out whether anyone had seen or heard from Tinkum. It was all he could do not to say more than he did with Olive standing there all puffed up and no plan other than a roaming dog.

Arvis thought too he would laugh himself sick when Henry got on quicker than anyone and sent her back across the field the way she came. Henry knew too that if Tinkum was ever going to find his way back home and stay put it wasn't going to be at the end of a woman's skirt. Tinkum had to find his own reasons for coming home and staying put. Arvis hoped the baby would be that reason.

With his hands too fidgety to get any work done, and missing Caroline more than words could say, Arvis decided to take a ride into town and find a distraction from his thoughts or a means of relieving them.

Chapter Eight

Arvis drove around the Square. He waved at familiar faces and hollered hello at those he knew from school and the ball fields. Seeing people he had known since childhood gave him a sense of direction. Sense of hope. Hope for the future. Immediately his mind turned back to what had been eating a hole in his brain since he picked up the telephone to call Caroline and instead lingered too long eavesdropping on Olive and Beatrix talking. Tinkum was going to be a daddy and didn't know it. The idea made the tiny hairs on his forearms straighten.

He had watched as Ram took to fatherhood. Those girls of his and Milly's were a handful to the most seasoned of fathers but Ram didn't see an ounce of trouble in them. Arvis's shins still smarted to think about how that oldest one, Della, kicked him black and blue when he was asked to fetch her from the backyard at last year's Decoration Day. To this day he still laughs thinking about how he threatened to put her in the dog pen if she didn't stop carrying on but it didn't do any good threatening her and it didn't slow her flailing. She was like any other woman he had ever known because by the time they got to the house she was all smiles and sunshine in her Sunday best. No one noticed Arvis limping around the cemetery that afternoon from the goose eggs she had just planted on his shins. He was thankful for it because who would show any mercy to a grown man whining over a little girl getting the best of him. He did his best to hide the pain as he carried flower arrangements and mowed the grass that afternoon at Huddy Hall Cemetery.

Turning out onto the state highway that ran up on the ridge, Arvis pushed his truck passed the legal speed limit giving the engine a good working out. The smell of impending rain filtered through the open vents and circulated throughout the cab. The tiny hairs on his forearms had relaxed coiling into tiny springs. He rolled his head from side to side releasing the tension that had been building in his neck rising from his shoulders. He had to get this news about Tinkum being a father off his mind and he had to do it quick.

Arvis decided he would leave things to chance. Stopping at Chilton's Service Station to fill up and grab a bottle of Coke and bag of peanuts, he decided who ever happened to be at the service station would be who he would tell. He knew it wasn't the best of plans but more times than not he had left the important things of his life to chance and more times than not they always worked out. Caroline was a perfect example and always his affirmation that he could trust chance to get him out of a sticky situation. Had it not been for betting on chance, he would never have asked Caroline to marry him.

Ram likes to take credit for it. He and Milly both like to say it was because of them that Arvis and Caroline are together. Because it was Ram and Milly that insisted on Arvis and Caroline partner up when they played any sort of game. Whether it was horseshoes or croquet or a hand of cards, they always played partners and Ram and Milly always insisted that Arvis and Caroline be partnered. But, Arvis knew the truth. He knew if it hadn't been for betting himself that if Caroline shot three out of four skeets at the Sunday school social he would never have asked her to let him give her a ride home. And, had she not said yes, all because she shot three out of the four skeets, he would never have had the nerve to ask her to go to the Dairy Dip. And, six months later asked her to marry him, all because she shot three out of four. Arvis trusted chance more than he trusted himself.

"What'll it be Arvis?" Roy Chilton asked pulling a grease stained shop rag from his back pocket. He wiped his hands with it and returned it to his pocket without looking.

"Fill 'er up. I reckon." Arvis said getting out of the truck. "Y'all got any cold ones in the cooler?" He asked knowing the answer.

"Filled her up this morning. Should be plenty in there and should be ice cold." Roy said adjusting the gasoline nozzle. "Just opened a bag of peanuts too. Help yourself. Came in from Georgia yesterday. Should be good ones. Got a whole barrel full this time around. Wonder how long they'll last us!" Roy shouted through his laughter at the back of Arvis making his way across the filling station parking lot to the office where the cold drink machine stood with a barrel of peanuts beside it.

Filling a brown paper sack half full of peanuts, Arvis opened his Coke bottle on the machines built in bottle opener leaving the cap on the floor where it landed. Resting his weight on the service counter, he shelled a handful of peanuts, took a long drink from his bottle, and emptied his fist full of peanuts into the bottle watching them float and the drink foam.

"Arvis! When are you going to do something about that tailgate on that truck?" Goldalena Filbry asked as she came through the service station door pushing it closed instead of letting it close on its own forcing the bell hanging above it to jingle twice.

Arvis groaned almost choking on his peanuts and Coke. He trusted chance to deliver him a confessor but chance was a cruel master sometimes and today was proving to be one of those times. Of all the people in Jessup County, who could possibly have walked through that day at that given moment, why it had to be Goldie was beyond anything Arvis could imagine. But, he had casted lots, and he was bound to keep to his plan. She would soon hear what he had to say. He just wasn't sure how he was going to get to it. Goldie Filbry had a knack for hijacking conversations and Arvis didn't have the patience to wait her out. But today had to be different.

"When are you going to quit nagging me about that tailgate Goldalena?" Arvis knew before the words made it out of his mouth, across the room, and into her ears that the look on her face was a sure indication that he was off on the wrong foot.

"Don't get smart with me Arvis Ange. You know better than anyone that tailgate has been hanging on by a thread for way too long. It falls off while you're on the ridge and you'll be sending someone off the edge. Mark my words, if you don't do something and do it soon, our next conversation will be at the jail." Goldie helped herself to a bottle of Coke and bag of peanuts.

Still leaning against the counter, too afraid to move and not having any desire to rest on one of the folding chairs lining the window of the service station office, Arvis bit his tongue with what he wanted to say in response. Instead he studied Roy Chilton washing the windshield and drying his hands on the shop towel from his back pocket. Giving Roy time to make his way back inside and ring up his gasoline, Arvis decided to give the service station owner the opportunity to figure out how to fasten the tailgate giving himself the opportunity to figure out how to unload his burden on the one person he would have never considered telling.

"Roy, before you tell me what I owe you. Want you to take a look at my tailgate. It needs bracing. See what you can do." Arvis said puffed up and watching as Roy's chest swelled too with pride and purpose. Out of the corner of his eye, he saw Goldie shaking her head. She wasn't buying the sudden demonstration of responsibility and all but bit her tongue in two not to say something she would later regret. Arvis knew and appreciated how hard it was for her to keep silent.

With Roy back out at the pickup truck and the only sound in the room was the sound of fan oscillating and peanuts crunching, Arvis turned his full attention on Goldie.

"Goldie, I need to talk to you." Arvis said with the sincerity of a preacher. He half expected her to burst out laughing spewing Coke and peanut pieces across the room but instead she just nodded.

Turning to lean sideways against the counter for comfort and keeping the advantage of seeing Goldie and Roy just over her shoulder out the big plate glass window, Arvis took a swig of Coke pushing the peanuts back into the bottle with his tongue.

"I've got something on my mind that I need to tell someone I can trust. And, well, I can't think of no one I trust more..." Arvis stopped short as Goldie's hand flew up.

"I'll stop you right there mister! You know just as well as I do you'll get a lot further along if you just get on with it. I don't need buttering up." Goldie said locking eyes with Arvis.

He nodded and continued, "Ahem, well, you see...it's like this..." He paused again. She sat patiently. Roy squatted behind the truck eyeballing the hinge. "there's going to be a baby."

With her hands resting on her crossed leg, Goldie didn't flinch, "Well, Arvis, what are you going to do about? You're already planning on getting married. Can't see anyone faulting you for getting in a hurry about things. Sounds like you just need to move up the date."

"Uh! What!? What are you talking about moving up the date?" Arvis said. His eyes the size of half dollars.

"Oh put your eyes back in your head, man. You think you're the only ones that ever got too friendly too soon and had to pay the consequences. Like I said, it ain't like you were already planning on getting married. Caroline knows as well as any woman you can take a wedding dress up but you can't let it out. She'll have to move the date whether she likes it or not." Goldie continued giving advice not once considering Arvis wasn't talking about himself.

His mind roamed from Tinkum and Beatrix and their baby to Caroline being round and full of life stuffed into a wedding dress pulling apart at the seams. He had barely managed to get a good night kiss out of her. How anyone could imagine he and Caroline could possibly be expecting was more than his mind could piece together. He hadn't even thought of it. He wondered now, if Caroline had.

"Arvis! Arvis! Are you listening to me?" Goldie shouted and then turned to see what had his attention outside. Roy had crawled into the truck bed and was spying the tailgate from the inside. If the boy couldn't fix it at least he could give a description of it if and when it came flying off landing God knows where.

"No. I mean yes. I mean. Not me. I'm not talking about me. Me and Caroline." Arvis said almost in a whisper. Something down deep inside of him broke in two and he didn't know why. The thought of him and Caroline not having children didn't feel right. Didn't sound right. Didn't settle right on his heart.

"Well if you ain't talking about y'all who are you talking about?"

"Tinkum. Tinkum and Bea are going to have a baby. And before you get all fired up about how I know and what business of it is mine, I don't have to tell you how bad this is with the way Tinkum can't seem to keep put for a week's worth of Sundays. And, I don't have to remind you, he ain't nowhere to be found right now." Arvis adjusted his weight on his feet. The weight of his confession adding to his discomfort instead of relieving him as he had intended.

Goldie studied her hands still resting on her crossed legs. The Coke bottle sweating leaving a ring on her shirtwaist dress. She turned the bottle to the left and then to the right. Her mind racing with all the places she had flushed Tinkum out of like covey of quail. She always believed the men, Ram, Arvis and her Henry knew where to find Tinkum but being men and not wanting to come between a man and his misery whether that misery was his woman or something else, they left Tinkum to his own devises and timing. But, she wasn't so inclined to leave the man to find his way back believing that if he was left stewing for too long he would forget how to come back or worse, he would make it impossible to come back. If Arvis didn't know where he was, and it sounded like that was the case, then it did her no good trying to find him. Maybe this time Tinkum was gone for good. But, Tinkum being gone wasn't the only problem here. Bea was having a baby and Tinkum or no Tinkum, she was in an uphill climb.

"I'm not going to bother asking how it is you know this. What's important right now is getting Bea the help she needs. Where's Olive? Last I saw her she was over at their place. Is she staying there now? Is that why she was there? She already knows?" Goldie paused. "Wait don't bother answering. I can tell by the look on your face I'm on the right track. Well, I can tell you right now, the last thing any of us need to do is tangle with Olive Pittman. If she is there then she is all the help Bea needs right now. You know how those two are. If you can get any closer than being twins those two have figured it out. You'd think they are the same person sometimes." Goldie stopped to take a drink and think through what to say and do next.

Arvis laughed, "You ever hear about that time Bea played a trick on Tinkum and sent Olive out on a date with him pretending to be Bea?" Arvis choked on a peanut hull laughing as he remembered the look on Tinkum's face when he found out he had been courting both sisters. He didn't notice that Goldie wasn't laughing. She knew the story and she didn't like it. Being a woman, she always believed there was more to that little mishap than two sisters playing a trick. She wouldn't put it past Olive to have masterminded the whole thing convincing Bea, if Bea had a choice or knew anything beforehand, to go in on the joke and that Tinkum would think it was funny too.

"Looks like you're going to need new hinges is all...I can order them and they'll more than likely be here this time next week. How's that work for you?" Roy asked as he marched through the office never seeing or hearing the conversation he interrupted. He made his way around behind the counter and began to ring up the gasoline and waited for Arvis to give the go ahead on the tailgate hinges.

"Order 'em!" Goldie said not giving Roy a chance to ask again.

"Yeah, I reckon you ought to go ahead and order 'em." Arvis said watching Roy press the cash register keys draining his wallet of its contents.

Chapter Nine

The St. Louis number nine rolled in to Union Station on the warmest day of spring Nashville had seen in weeks. George Gilford Taggart, Sr., folded the newspaper he had been pretending to read for the last several miles, placed it under his arm and gathered his coat, hat and bags before shuffling out with the rest of the passengers. Looking over the shoulder of the stout woman in front of him, the one with the scented drug store powder that had been permeating the train car since Paducah, Kentucky, he tried to time his departure with that of the irritating salesman in the gray pinstripe that had been chewing his ear off for the last hour. Taggart appreciated a good sales pitch. He had been the top earning salesman for Southeastern Feed and Seed the last four years running. But, it wasn't the man's pitch that grated on Taggart's nerves. Not the sales pitch. It was the pitch of his voice. Just over six feet in his stocking feet and well over two hundred pounds in his birthday suit, Taggart's voice had been compared to the mellow drone of an upright bass. He didn't mind the sound of his own voice and took great pleasure in exercising it but the little oily haired East Tennessean in the gray pin stripe and his nasal whine was unbearable. George Gilford Taggart was bound and determined not to waste another minute of his already stretched schedule and patience listening to the man whine about the price of a cup of coffee and the lack of respect he had received from the good women of the Commonwealth of Kentucky regarding their interest in his demonstration of Electrolux's latest vacuum cleaner model.

Walking out of Union Station and onto Broadway, Taggart chewed his bottom lip and studied his pocket watch. Rosalee had never been late. In all the years she had dropped him off at the train station and picked him up again, he had never done what he did today. After departing the train he paced the aisle looking this way and that for any sign of his wife and child. She always was there. There at the bench nearest to the tracks waiting and watching. But not today. Resolved that she was nowhere to be found in the train station, he walked outside to see if maybe she was on her way. Half expecting to see her running toward the train station the boy in tow certain she was later than she expected, Taggart couldn't believe his eyes when the only thing he saw on the sidewalk was the skinny East Tennessean tossing his bags and samples in the trunk of a taxi.

Not to be outdone by anyone, including his wife, George Gilford Taggart, Sr., watched as the taxi rolled by and the whiny voiced salesman looked the other way as another taxi took its place. Taggart climbed into the back, his coat, hat and bag tucked in beside him where his family should have been, and gave the driver his address.

The short five mile drive from Union Station to his home was not enough time and distance for Taggart to reason through why his wife and child were not there to meet him. Neither was it enough time for his pride to simmer allowing him the courage to return to the station if the car wasn't at home. The taxi pulled up to the curb and Taggart paid the fare without saying a word, got out of the car with his belongings and stared at the cold dark house and the empty garage.

Fishing through his pockets for the front door key and then remembering he never traveled with it because Rosalee was always with him when he returned from his sales trips, Taggart began to feel the weight of his expectations. Tipping the flowerpot over, he found the extra key, entered and closed the door behind him.

"Rosalee!" Taggart had to try. Try calling out to her. Giving her benefit of the doubt. Maybe she forgot what day it was. Maybe she forgot what time it was. Maybe she forgot where she was supposed to be.

"George!" Taggart called out for his son as he opened and closed the boy's bedroom door finding it just as it had been earlier in the week when they left for the train station together. Every toy in place. Every shoe. Every jacket. Everything that proved there had been a boy in the home was right where it belonged except for the boy.

Taggart searched every room of the small house looking for something to tell him what had happened. Something to tell him where his family was. Sitting on the side of the bed he shared with Rosalee, George Gilford Taggart came to the realization that he had taken too much for granted. Wherever his wife and child were, they managed to get there without him.

Not one for being overly emotional or irrational, Taggart decided to work with what he did knew until he could figure out what he didn't know. First things first, he was hungry. The stale coffee and donut he had at midday was not enough to sustain him any longer. Whether he wanted to admit it to himself, his emotions had taken a toll on him and stripped him of physical resources too.

Leaning on the refrigerator door, the light casting a yellow beam across the dark kitchen, Taggart drank from the milk bottle and gathered what he needed for a cheese sandwich. A can of Spam and a Beefsteak tomato quickly followed the cheese sandwich along with two fingers of Tennessee whiskey. A car door slammed outside and Taggart rushed to the living room window in time to see his neighbor from across the street walking up her front sidewalk, her arms full of grocery sacks.

"Doris! Let me help you with that!" Taggart shouted as he trotted across the street to the woman standing and waiting.

"Oh I appreciate that. These things get heavier it seems once they get home." Doris said. "There you go, just put them down there on the counter. Can I get you a cup of coffee for your trouble?"

"Coffee sounds good but no trouble. No trouble at all." Taggart said as he pulled a stool up to the kitchen counter just on the other side of the wall of brown grocery bags. "I was just getting in and happened to see you wrestling these things inside. What you got going on here? Planning a big party?"

Taggart could count on his hand the number of times he had spoken two words to his neighbor but he had an ulterior motive and it wasn't for her trying to be neighborly that had kept him from walking over sooner.

Laughing Doris said, "No. I like to stock up. You know. Can goods go on sale. Four for this. Three for that. You just never know when you're going to need a can of something and I like knowing I've got a can or two of whatever it may be in the pantry. Some may call it wasteful but I call it prepared."

"Nah, that ain't wasteful at all. I agree. You're planning ahead. Nothing wrong with that from where I'm sitting." Taggart smiled and added two spoons of sugar to his coffee.

"Is that how Rosalee does it?" Doris asked behind her cup of coffee.

"Does what?"

"Can goods. You know. The groceries. Is that how Rosalee does it? Does she plan ahead?"

Taggart sat for a moment not sure how to answer. He had no idea how Rosalee did anything. Not that it mattered how he answered Doris. She was a means to an end. It didn't matter to him if he told her Rosalee plans months in advance or that she swings from the end of her apron strings running out of everything before replacing it. To him the truth wasn't what was at stake here. At least not the truth about Rosalee's grocery habits. The truth he was seeking was if Doris knew anything about Rosalee's whereabouts. And, by the look and sound of things, she didn't.

George Gilford Taggart had prided himself on being able to read any given situation and he was reading from Doris and this conversation about purchasing habits that she had no idea Rosalee was not at home this very minute. His sales experience may be with men unlike the East Tennessee vacuum salesman but people are all the same. Male or female. If they know something, more times than not, they will let you know what they know. Sometimes even when they don't realize they are saying anything at all. That's what he was looking for with Doris. A passing comment. A slip of the tongue. Something from her that would point him the direction of Rosalee and his son.

"Well, I better get back across the street and let you put these things away. I appreciate the coffee. Sure was good. Better than that stuff you get on the road." Taggart said as he politely made his way back toward her front door.

"Yeah, I guess you'd know about those sorts of things. Being gone so much and all." Doris said stepping out onto her front porch as her neighbor walked down her sidewalk.

"Thank you again." Taggart said. His last ditch effort to get a response. A reaction.

"Tell Rosalee I want to hear all about her trip when she gets back. I guess it's been close to five maybe six years since I was in Chattanooga. Guess my sister thinks I've all but disowned her. I told Rosalee she should look her up while she's there." Doris said just as her neighbor was about to cross the street.

George Gilford Taggart stopped dead in his tracks.

Chapter Ten

Sweat rolled off George Taggart's face as he dropped box after box from the attic to the hallway floor. He wanted to cuss. Cuss Rosalee for forcing him to go to such extreme measures to find her. Cuss Doris for giving him just enough information to send him on this wild goose chase. And, cuss himself, for not having better control over his house that his wife could run off with no trace.

Mercury glass Christmas ornaments shattered inside the boxes from being dropped. George knew if the shoe was on the other foot, if Rosalee was having to go through boxes to find a scrap of paper to point her in the direction he had gone, she would feel the same way he does now. Numb. Part of him hated that he was destroying their memories. Memories wrapped up in tissue paper and stored in corrugated boxes for nine out of the twelve months of the year. But, if memories were what was holding them together, they had been shattered long before George dropped the first box from the attic.

It's got to be here! He thought. Doris wouldn't have been so obvious about mentioning her sister and making the point in reminding him, not so subtly, she owned the other dry cleaning store. He remembered when the card came in the mail last year. He actually thought it was a genius move. Offer a discount on dry cleaning on the postcard styled Christmas card to be redeemed at either of the family owned and operated dry cleaning stores. He still remembers the argument he and Rosalee had over keeping the card instead of redeeming it at the one Doris owned in Nashville for his white shirts. They were forever sending an arm load of dress white shirts to her store, why not take advantage of the holiday generosity and use the discount. Just this once. But Rosalee didn't want to part with the card. She insisted the card was more for the holiday and less for business. It was then, like many times before, that George realized just how limited Rosalee's thinking was. But then again, as he sat in the middle of his hallway, sorting through broken ornaments and stacks and stacks of Christmas cards saved from year to year, he began to wonder if maybe she had hatched her plan last year and was waiting for the right moment. Had she taken advantage of the discount by using the card, she wouldn't have it later when she needed the address and calling card so to speak for showing up unannounced and unplanned at the Chattanooga business. That is if it was unannounced and unplanned. The more George thought about it the more he began to wonder if maybe Doris was sitting across the street in her butterscotch colored kitchen filled with canned goods having a good laugh at his expense. Was this something these three women had been cooking up all along? Had Rosalee confided in Doris who then confided in her sister who then suggested maybe even insisted that Rosalee come to Chattanooga and start a new life? George had heard of things like this. He hadn't travel the line from St. Louis to Nashville all these years and not come across all walks of life. He just never thought he would be dealing with this sort of thinking in his own home.

Shuffling through Christmas cards, he came across the postcard from last year. Merry Christmas and a phone number were scratched in fountain pen. Studying the card, George wasn't sure if he dared dialing the number or try to work it into conversation with Doris. He would have to sleep on this one. This was something he couldn't rush. He had no idea what exactly he was dealing with and had even less of an idea what to do about it.

Running scenarios out in his head, George thought about catching the next train to Chattanooga but where exactly would he go first. The dry cleaners? He had no real proof where she was. The more he thought about that the more he realized he was grasping at straws. He really had no proof she went to Chattanooga. Or that Doris or her sister was involved. He had built a whole strategy based on one comment. He no longer felt like himself. The desperation was too uncomfortable. His world had turned upside down and he couldn't turn it right side up again.

Deciding to handle this the way he handled a sale, he tackled first things first. He was still hungry. The sun had already set draining the house of light. The single light over the kitchen sink was not enough light to fill the space he now occupied in the hall. Leaving the boxes and cards and shards of ornaments, George pushed himself up off the hardwood floor of the hallway. Left the ladder pulled down from the attic and forged through the kitchen for something to fill his stomach.

The smell of coffee soothed his worried mind. Sipping slowly, he flipped the dry cleaners postcard over and over in his hand. The telephone number appeared to grow in size the longer he looked at it. He knew he was imagining it. He knew he was making more of the number than it deserved. But, he knew if he didn't decide to take action, he would never get sleep.

Buying himself some time before jumping into action just because he didn't want to look back on this moment and regret he didn't take his time. Always feeling the need to be in charge, even when he was the only one in the room, George delayed his plan until he had something to eat.

Finding a sleeve of crackers, he crushed them into a bowl and poured the last of the milk over them. He ate slowly and deliberately until it was all gone. Washing the last bite down with another cup of black coffee, George traced the telephone number with his finger and then carried the card out to hallway where the phone rested in the niche.

Holding his breath waiting as the slow rumble of the long distance connection echoed through the ear piece, George closed his eyes and waited. Waited for someone to answer. A voice in his head quickly reminded him it was after business hours just in case the number was the dry cleaner's telephone number. Instinctively, George opened his eyes to ward off the accusatory voice and prove it wrong as he read again for the umpteenth time, the telephone number listed under the street address and store hours. The handwritten number was not the same.

"Posey's, how can I help you?" The voice broke the rumble and static.

George panicked. He had not thought of what to say if and when someone picked up on the other end. He wanted to believe it was just going to ring. Truth be told, he didn't want to know the answer to the swarm of questions buzzing around inside of his head. But, here he was connected to someone through this year-old Christmas postcard.

Clearing his throat and trying desperately to come up with something to say, George asked the obvious. It was out of his mouth before he had time to think it through and decide if it was the best option or not. "Rosalee Taggart please." He asked with a calm assurance that truly escaped him. He wasn't sure where the confidence came from that filled his voice.

"Rose you say?" The voice asked.

"Yes, please. Is she there? I'd like to speak with her." George asked allowing the person on the other end to assume they were talking about the same person. It was his only hope and his only course of action at the moment. Sure it could have been a complete mistake but he had to try.

The long pause concerned him. If the voice on the other end asked who was calling or what his business was with Rose, he wasn't sure what would come flying from his mouth. He had not planned on anything before the call and his own actions were surprising him as much as they would be surprising anyone else.

Pressing his ear to the ear piece trying to make out the muffled conversation taking place on the other end. A conversation in the room but not close enough to the telephone to make out just what was being said but certain it had everything to do with who this person knew as Rose. And who this person assumed the caller was asking for named Rose.

"Excuse me? Hello?" George said trying to move the voice along.

"Yes, that's right. I'm here. Rose you say?" The voice asked but didn't wait for the reply. "She is working today. Mrs. Posey believes she will be back at the boarding house by the time for George's bath but not sooner. I suppose we won't be seeing her at dinner tonight." The voice added the last part as a reminder to himself and less as information for the caller. "Can I leave her your name? I believe there's something to write on here by the telephone. I can't say I would remember more than a name if that considering she is going to be a while getting back here. If you'll give me a minute or two I can go fetch a pen and paper and take down your message." And with that the voice walked away from the telephone leaving George to wonder if he would return.

Not wanting to leave any information and doubting the voice would remember the call in the first place, George placed the ear piece on the cradle and returned to the kitchen stepping over and around Christmas boxes with more satisfaction than he did just an hour earlier. Resting in his chair at the kitchen table, enjoying the last of the coffee, George felt very satisfied with himself and his telephone call.

The number was to a boarding house. Posey was the name the voice gave when he answered. He called Rosalee, Rose. George was use to that – it happened more often than he knew and he knew it happened often. Rosalee was forever explaining her name was Rosalee and not Rose Lee. It would appear that problem followed her to Chattanooga.

Tracing his finger over the number again this time he wondered if it had anything to do with the dry cleaners or if like many times before the card just happened to be nearby when a piece of paper was needed to jot down a number. Studying the handwriting, George decided the card came with the number on it or it was added by someone other than Rosalee because like his wife's familiar hairstyle and choice of perfume, George Taggart knew his wife's handwriting and this wasn't it.

Placing the dirty dishes in the kitchen sink and looking out to the dark house across the street. George knew the next move was to get more information out of Doris. He didn't know just how he was going to manage it because he had spent so many years avoiding the woman's company. But, he knew he would come up with something and considering he was on the right track, he knew that something would find him soon enough.

Chapter Eleven

The dog days of summer rolled over the ridge sinking suffocating heat deep into the hollows. Window screens that had billowed with sweet fragrant breezes of honeysuckle and Carolina jasmine only months earlier now sagged in desperation for relief from the humidity. Sweating that would eventually turn to rust.

Beatrix fanned herself with a Bishop's Funeral Home fan. The bed covers rolled in a ball at the foot of the bed reeked of damp and perspiration. Her head ached from the sweltering temperature inside the house but she had been bedridden since Dr. Bass told her four months ago that she was pregnant. He refused to allow her to leave the bed for anything other than to use the slop jar. The slop jar souring under the foot of the bed. The bed she had slept in, ate in, and cried in for the last few months waiting and wondering and worrying where her husband had run off to and if and when he would be coming home. He didn't know about the baby. He didn't know that she had carried it this long. He didn't know that if she did as the doctor insisted, he would soon be a daddy.

A fly buzzed around the room. Just as the buzzing fell silent, Beatrix heard a car door slam. She had been expecting Dr. Bass but it could have been Olive back from her errands in town. Beatrix looked forward to seeing the doctor and hearing how well she and the baby were progressing but she had set her mouth to the taste of watermelon ever since Olive mentioned she was going to town and would bring home anything Beatrix needed or wanted. Olive had made a few dollars working a shift at the crate factory in Fulton despite her father's opinions of women working outside the home. Fletcher Pittman was full of opinions and never at a loss for sharing them. He railed on Olive and Beatrix to depend solely on the provision of a man and not their own means to keep a roof over their heads and food on the table. Olive knew her father meant well and she didn't disagree that a husband was the head of the house and the provider but when she didn't have a husband and when her sister's husband was nowhere to be found, she believed it fell upon her to make sure there was a roof and food. Besides, if she and her twin sister started gee-hawing to their daddy's demands this late in life, he just might keel over dead. Whether Fletcher Pittman liked it or not, Olive would do whatever she had to do to keep her sister comfortable at least until she had the baby. After that, well, Olive decided she'd cross that bridge when she got to it.

"Yo, in the house! Beatrix!" Dr. Bass called as he climbed the two rickety porch steps in need of repair.

Beatrix leaned over the side of the bed to see him standing at the screen door. Olive had moved the bed into the front room two weeks after she moved in making the excuse that Beatrix would be comfortable and feel like she was more a part of things if she was in the front room in the bed instead of tucked away in the bedroom. And, after a couple of weeks of sleeping on a pallet of quilts on the bedroom floor, Olive moved her bed from her childhood home to Tinkum and Bea's. Just one more tangle she had to endure with Fletcher and his need to keep things like they always had been. Change had always been and would always be an enemy to Fletcher Pittman.

"Hey Dr. Bass! Come on in." Beatrix eased up onto the bed pillows brushing her sweat soaked hair back off her forehead. Her braid was unraveling and her hands instinctively moved to repair the damage. Her eyes followed the doctor's as she watched him watch her unbraid and braid her long strawberry blonde hair tying the end with a blue grosgrain ribbon.

The doctor's face flushed. His eyes followed her hands. Her long tapered fingers weaving the rosy tendrils. The bow faded periwinkle resting on pin tuck pleats stretched open from her engorged breasts. Throughout his long medical career, Dr. Bass had seen the terrible and the terrific of what the human body could render but it was in the small graceful movements of a woman where he found the most pleasure.

"You here by yourself?" He asked peeling his eyes away from Beatrix and looking around the small room and making a show of looking out the windows. He knew from absence of Olive's car not being outside that she was not at home and he had just been next door looking in on Milly Hatch and her fifth pregnancy to know that Tinkum had not returned home. Milly was forever changing the subject from herself and Ephraim and the girls to what was going on with everyone else. Especially, what was going on next door and Dr. Bass hoped it was out of a sense of compassion and not gossip but he doubted it was.

Sighing for no other reason than being bored with the subject Beatrix said, "Yes," and made an effort to sit up on the side of the bed.

"No. No. We don't need you making any show of getting up. You've done good to stay put and that's what we need you to keep doing." Dr. Bass said placing his hands on her shoulders and coaxing her back onto the pillows. "Now, let's take a listen and see how this feller is doing."

Rubbing his hands together and then rubbing the end of his stethoscope on his pant leg to warm them, he gazed off into the distance as though he was seeing some invisible scene play out in the center of the room. Smiling. Nodding. And clearing his throat for effect if nothing else. He coiled the stethoscope on itself and tucked it back into his black bag.

"Tell me. How are you feeling?" He asked as he continued to sit on the side of the bed more like an old friend coming to call for a visit and less like the physician at the county hospital.

"I reckon I'm fair to middlin'. Can't complain." Beatrix said with a slight pout.

He watched the supple freckled skin of her neck pulse harder.

"That's good. Now, tell me. What's on your mind?" He asked placing his hand on the bed beside his black bag and adjusting his weight to rest on his arm now arched over her knees.

Beatrix liked the coziness and the attention but didn't understand it. She peddled her feet back and forth as her mind raced to find an answer to his question.

"I. I don't know. First one thing then another, I reckon. Just like any woman, I suppose." She said blushing and staring at her feet still peddling back and forth.

Reaching back with his hand, Dr. Bass stilled her feet and left his hand on them as he asked again, "Tell me. What's on your mind?"

A knot of emotion swelled in her throat and tears flooded her eyelids brimming but not falling. She stared at his hand and thought of Tinkum. She missed him. Missed his touch. His voice. His confidence that everything would work out in the end. She needed him more than she wanted to admit.

"Beatrix, it's not enough that you stay in the bed. It's not enough that you rest your body. Hon, you have to rest your mind too. That little feller feels everything you're feeling. If you stayed tied up inside fretting over first one thing then another, he is too. And, I know you don't want that, am I right?"

They both nodded.

"So tell me what's on your mind. Maybe it's something I can fix or find someone who can. Or at least, it will get it off your mind and if nothing else, free you and this little man up from the weight of it."

His hand moved from her feet to her round belly and then back to the place next to his medical bag.

"I just don't know where to begin and I'm afraid once I get started I won't know where to end." Beatrix said as she took a deep breath and just as she was about to open her mouth and her heart she and the doctor were distracted by the screen door opening.

"Well how's our patient?" Olive asked. Her arms wrapped around two brown paper grocery sacks.
Dr. Bass jumped into motion grabbing the sacks and searching for a place to put them. Following Olive, he situated them onto the small table against the wall between the cook stove and the back door. Appearing more animated than before, he relayed his standing orders to Olive to keep her sister as calm and as still as possible only allowing her to leave the bed to relieve her bladder or bowels and to call him immediately if there was any sign of pain or bleeding.

Olive busied herself emptying the grocery sacks dismissing the doctor more with her silence than anything else and giving him every indication that she had things under control and that he was free to go on his way.

Beatrix watched from the bed as she did everything in silence and disappointment. He had come to see her and see her he did until Olive entered the room and swallowed all the air out of it. Deflated, Beatrix sat slumped shouldered against the moist pillows and hoped that the doctor would assume his previous position on the bed but instead he made no eye contact and he made no comment as he reached across her for his black bag and walked out of the house in silence.

"I just don't understand that man." Olive said folding the brown paper sacks. "You'd think the way he marches in here every four weeks or so and repeats the same old tired instructions that he did the last time that he must think we don't have the sense of frog between us. Does he think we're stupid or what?"

Beatrix knew better than to engage Olive when she was in one of her moods. She knew this had nothing to do with her or the doctor or what if anything he thought of her or her sister. Beatrix knew from experience and being an identical twin that something or better yet someone happened while Olive was out in town and it would only be a matter of time before Beatrix heard the whole story. She had learned the hard way as a child not to comfort Olive before she was ready for comfort. Like a scalded cat, Olive Ann Pittman could slice the skin of the best intentioned soul if they came too close too soon. It was best to wait her out.

Three short rings from the telephone sent Olive across the room and to the telephone receiver.

"Hell-o. Well it's about dang time. You know I was just right there. Why in the world you couldn't have taken the time to climb down off that dang tractor then instead of waiting until I got all the way home. Al-right! Al-right I said. I'll be right there. Hold your horses." Slamming the receiver onto the cradle, Olive grabbed her keys and shouted back over her shoulder as the screen door whipped closed behind her, "That was Arvis. I'll be right back."

Beatrix was certain Olive was swearing all the way to the car and if she could see past the front porch and down the road from her perch on the bed she was certain she would have seen her sister still cussing a blue streak all the way up the hollow.

Slipping out of the bed, Beatrix fingered through the remaining grocery sack left standing on the side table. Coffee, sugar, flour, a bag of beans and an empty Hershey's chocolate bar wrapper. No watermelon. None to be seen. Not from either of the two sacks. Once again, Olive had forgotten the one thing she said she would do. The one and only reason she said she was running to town to get her sister what she wanted. To get her a watermelon.

Easing back into the bed, but not before spying out the window and across the tobacco field at Ram Hatch kicking up a cloud of dust behind his pickup truck probably rushing to town to get Milly a slice of lemon merengue pie from the diner or a quart of buttermilk from the store or whatever she happened to mention in passing because that's what husbands do. And if you don't have a husband on hand, a sister should.

Chapter Twelve

The sharp smell of axil grease competed with curtain of darkness housing unseen insects and nocturne animals in the high ceiling barn with its two bay doors on either end neither offering enough sunlight to see two steps in front of you. Arvis had left the tractor just outside the road side barn doors but was working his way through a tattered box of parts at the workbench at the pasture side barn doors. The tractor was burning oil faster than he could keep it filed and he needed to open her up and see what was causing the problem. He had been looking for his pliers when he got distracted by the box of parts and decided to rummage through it.

Olive panned the fields looking for Arvis as she came down the hollow passing the Ange fields before getting to the barns and then the house at the end of the road. Seeing the tractor parked outside of the long narrow barn, she pulled her car up beside it and kicked her way through the tall grass hoping not to come up on a snake. Arvis was the only snake in the grass she had any intentions of dealing with today.

"Where's my watermelon you big lug!" She shouted into the barn not daring to venture into its cavernous belly.

"Woman, you call me a slug again and I'll show you where you can find a watermelon." Arvis volleyed back trying to sound more playful than hurtful. He didn't care for Olive and had no intentions in locking horns with her but she could bring the worst out of anyone in no time flat.

Laughing that her words were misunderstood but their meaning wasn't she waited for him to finish what he was doing and give her the attention and the watermelon she demanded.

Reaching the bottom of the box but still more fascinated with its contents than Olive Pittman, Arvis maintained his focus on his work leaving Olive to stew in her own juices. If he couldn't get the best of her with his words, he would defeat her, if not frustrate her, with his silence.

"Guess you heard about Tinkum?" Olive said after several minutes of nothing but the sound of grease filled fingernails scraping the bottom of the weathered pasteboard box. Metal tractor parts tumbling.

Arvis laughed. His round shoulders bouncing causing his galluses to pull tight. He knew she didn't know anything about Tinkum that he wouldn't know first. He let her stew a little longer just for fun and to see just how long it would take her before her pride sent her through the barn.

Shifting her weight from one foot to the other while keeping her eyes on Arvis and the tall grass around her feet expecting movement from either place, Olive cleared her throat and with her hands on her hips said, "Well, I guess if you don't care nothing about it I can go talk to Caroline. I'm sure she'd be more than interested in knowing."

With one swing of his arm, Arvis sent the box of parts sailing across the barn and crashing against the wall. The explosion of tractor parts kept Arvis from hearing Caroline say hello. The blinding anger and dark barn kept him from seeing her standing just behind Olive. Olive didn't turn to see her but knew she was there and took full advantage of the situation. No one heard or saw Goldalena Filbry standing just behind Arvis. She, like Caroline, had come to talk to Arvis. But, unlike Caroline, Goldie was not interested in making her visit known to anyone but Arvis. She had topped the hill just in time to see Caroline getting out of her car. Leaving her car parked at the top of the hill, Goldie walked through the pastures, around behind the barns hoping to stay out of sight until the women were gone. She knew she was taking a chance in either one of them seeing her car parked just off the road at the cattle gate but that was a risk she was willing to take. It had been four long months since Arvis unloaded his burden on her at Chilton's Service Station without any more news from Arvis or Henry about how Beatrix was doing or if Tinkum had returned. Before she started questioning her husband and disrupt the delicate balance of her marital bliss, she wanted to go to the source. Arvis Ange.

Arvis braced himself two-handed on the workbench. He wanted to grab Olive by the throat and silence her once and for all. Do everyone a favor. But, the workbench would have to do.

"I just wanted to stop by and let you know the Bea and the baby are doing fine. She appreciates you sending her the watermelon. Said it was sweet of you to take care of her cravings like that. Said you're about as sweet as your watermelons." Olive's voice echoed through the barn. It's sing song tone unlike the venomous greeting she spewed minutes earlier. Unlike the greeting, her words now had a much more interesting and engaged audience. More than she knew.

Caroline stopped cold in her tracks when she heard the words Bea and baby. A cold sweat flushed her warm skin. Her hands began to tremble. Her knees threatened to buckle. Her ears shut out all other sound as the words Bea and baby swarmed around and around inside her head. She wanted to run. She wanted to cry. She wanted to do anything but stand there falling apart as this ill-mannered woman shouted for God and everyone to hear that her husband-to-be was taking care of the mother of his child.

Goldalena Filbry pressed her back to the barn and her hand to her mouth forcing her lungs to stop drawing in air and forcing her ears to hear everything her eyes couldn't see. Anger coursed through her veins filling every extremity with enough determination and fortitude. She believed she could whip Arvis into next week and still have enough fight in her to rip Olive Pittman's tongue from its root.

Satisfied she had done enough to settle an unspoken score, Olive turned to get in her car never acknowledging Caroline standing nearby. Pulling out on the gravel road, Olive drove down to the house where two watermelons waited for her in the shade of the front porch. She knew she could have bypassed the barn all together and gone straight to where Arvis said he would leave the watermelons for her when he called her but what fun was in doing just that when there was so much more she could accomplish for Beatrix and for herself by stopping at the barn and stirring up a little trouble or fun depending on who you asked.

Caroline stood frozen watching Arvis mange to pull himself together a wall of silence and darkness separating them. Goldie exhaled quietly then pushed a mouthful of fresh air deep into her lungs. She refused to move until she knew Caroline had left too.

Voices filtered through the barn soft and low and masked by the sound of gravel crunching under car tires and the bleat of a car horn as Olive tried to have the last word. Goldie missed what was said between Arvis and Caroline. She wondered if they heard each other. A car door closed. A car engine hummed. And gravel crunched again but this time there was no bleating horn.

"How long you been standing there?" Arvis mumbled just above a whisper. His voice breaking with emotion.

"Long enough." Goldie said searching his face for answers but looking away when none were found.

Walking through the dark barn and back out to the waiting tractor, Arvis didn't see, hear or care that Goldie followed him.

"I just don't know what to say Arvis. It's been four going on five months since you told me about Bea expecting and not once did you think to tell me anymore than that. And don't come off now saying how there wasn't more to tell or that you figured Henry would have finished your tale for you. Best thing for you is to not bring Henry into this." Goldie scolded.

"Can't make you any promises there." Arvis said kicking at the tractor tires. Lost in thought.

Without any further discussion, Arvis climbed onto the tractor, started its engine and drove across the pasture and deep into the hollow behind a wall of pines leaving Goldie where she stood.

Chapter Thirteen

Goldie's hands shook uncontrollably as she did her best to mash the potatoes. Henry would be home soon and she had never been late getting supper on the table and she wasn't about to start tonight. She knew she couldn't just come right out and ask him about Arvis and Beatrix and the baby. She knew it wasn't right to put him on the spot or to ask him to betray a confidence. And, she knew in a sense she was bound by a confidence with Arvis to keep his secret. All afternoon she wrecked her brain trying to piece together everything he had said to her that day at Chilton's. He was never someone she cared to spend too much time with and she rarely gave two seconds of time to anything he said because it rarely added up to two cents worth anything anyone should care about until now. Now of all times when he finally said something she would care very much about knowing she couldn't remember just how it was he told her.

For the life of her, she had spent the last few months thinking she had been told Tinkum and Beatrix were having a baby. She had spent all these weeks getting all riled up over Tinkum Price high tailing it out of town again at the first sign of trouble when the trouble had stood at the counter of Chilton's Service Station floating peanuts in a Coke bottle not thinking twice before unburdening himself to her.

She had to think and think fast on what or how she could bring Henry around to talking about Beatrix or Tinkum or Arvis or the baby without Henry suspecting or believing or accusing her of meddling in things she had no business in or suggesting he knew more than he did. It had been a day of risks. Risks she was willing to take.

Setting the table and putting the supper dishes in the oven to stay warm, Goldie poured two fingers of whiskey with a splash of water in a glass and sipped on it slowly waiting for Henry to come through the door. She would pour him a drink too but no point in pouring it before he was ready to drink it. That looked contrived and she drew the line at appearing disingenuous.

"Nothing more a man appreciates than to come home to a loving woman." Henry said dropping his briefcase and taking

Goldie into his arms. Kissing her. "And there's nothing like a wet whiskey kiss. Pour me one, won't you?"

Warmed by the whiskey and the kiss, Goldie complied without question. Henry loosened his tie, peeled his suit coat off, and rolled his shirt sleeves while easing his shoes off toe to heel. It had been one of those days when he counted the hours. He knew opening his own law office in a small town, the same small town that saw him grow from a minnow to a big fish, would at times cost him blood, sweat and tears, but he never factored in the long days of silence and boredom. Being at home with his loving wife was all he needed to set the world back on its axis.

Goldie poured Henry a whiskey and refilled her glass before sliding between his legs to sit on his lap. "Well that's a welcome any man would appreciate." Henry said between sips.

Goldie looked into his blue eyes through the empty end of her glass.

"How was your day?" She asked with a slight slur.

Henry laughed. He had a gift for reading people and he was especially gifted at reading his wife. Something was up and it was only a matter of time or whiskey before she let loose and filled in the missing pieces.

"Today was like yesterday and the day before that and if I'm as smart as they say..." Henry stopped talking long enough for Goldie to remove her fingers from his lips as she shushed him. Laughing still, he finished, "...tomorrow..." he laughed harder as she upended his glass to her mouth with it still in his hand, "...will be the same."

"Uhm?" Shaking her head and tossing her curls. "I don't understand. What happened?" Goldie asked with a hiccupped.

"Goldie, why don't you tell me about your day?" Henry asked setting the empty glasses on the kitchen table in front of them.

Resting her head on his chest to still the room from spinning and to avoid his piercing blue eyes, Goldie shared how she had spent the morning making donuts and decided to take a dozen out to Beatrix Price. She reminded Henry without accusation that they had not stopped in to see Beatrix the last time they were at Ram and Milly's and with Tinkum out of town, again, she thought the visit was well overdue. Going on to tell him that while she was there she took some clothes off the line for Bea, folded them and put them away. And, tried to do what she could around the house so that Beatrix didn't feel like things were piling up waiting for her to feel better. She confessed to Henry that she waited the respectable amount of time before saying anything about what present illness had set her bedridden again making every effort not to suggest in any way that she could be contagious knowing all the while there was no way on God's green earth anyone could catch pregnancy. And it was then, when she said pregnancy. When that word entered the room. Ballooning in size. Pushing everything out of its way. Staring them both in the face. It was then that she knew she had gone too far. Gone too far with Beatrix. Gone too far with Henry. They knew that she knew. And if she knew, who else knew.

***

"Bea! I can't fix what's not broken!" Olive pleaded with her sister.

Beatrix cried. Tears failing like rain landing in a puddle of watermelon juice in the bowl resting in her lap.

"How can you say that? I told you twice already! She knows! And if she knows who else knows?"

"What does it matter who knows? Goldie Filbry. Arvis Ange. Or the Easter Bunny. Sister you're expecting a baby. That secret can't stay secret forever!"

"Arvis Ange? Why would you bring him up?" Beatrix screamed through her tears.

"Oh my stars! What does it matter whose name I said? Arvis Ange. Caroline Gentry. The Tooth Fairy! They are all going to know soon enough!"

"Caroline Gentry?" Beatrix wailed.

Grabbing the bowl of watermelon rinds, seeds and juice from her sister's lap praying it didn't get turned over making for yet another mess she didn't want to clean up tonight, Olive tossed the contents out the back door knowing she would regret it next spring when she would be forever pulling watermelon vines up from the roots.

"Listen to me Bea. It doesn't matter. Honey, it really doesn't. You're going to be a mama. Did you hear me? You – are – going – to – be – a – m-a-m-a. Let that sink in. I'm not going to let anyone take that away from you. Understand? Now, lay back there. Wipe your eyes and while you're at it wipe your nose," she paused waiting for Beatrix to laugh at the joke. She did. "And do what the doctor said do. Rest. Rest your body and your mind. I'm here to take care of you and everything else."

Beatrix did as her sister said.

"Now, that's it. Get some sleep. Everything will look better in the morning."

"Ollie?"

Olive stopped cleaning up and waited for her sister to say what was on her mind. To finish her sentence and fall asleep.

"Find him. Find Tinkum."

***

Olive sat on the stump outside the backdoor of the Red Stagg Tavern smoking her last cigarette and waiting for Red Connors to close the beer joint for the night. The moon was high in the sky and cinder block building was cooling from the heat it had absorbed during the day.

"Olive!" Red shouted dropping the crate of empty beer bottles and losing the few dollars he expected to get on returning them.

"Quieten down Red! You're going to wake the dead!"

"What are you doing out here? No wait. I know. Tinkum. Woman if I told you once, I've told you a hundred times. He ain't here."

Rubbing the fire off the cigarette against the bottom of her shoe, Olive followed Red back inside the tavern. Taking a seat at the bar she emptied half-eaten bowls of pretzels and nuts into one and began emptying it one pretzel and one nut at a time staving off the hollowness eating a hole in her stomach. Her nerves were getting the best of her stealing her ability to hold down a full meal and causing her to eat bits and pieces throughout the day to keep from wasting away from hunger.

"Beer?" Red asked opening a bottle of Falls City and placing it in front of her.

Turning the bottle up and downing a third in one swallow, Olive filled her mouth with pretzels to cut the aftertaste.

"Easy there or I'll be cleaning up more than peanut hulls off the floor. There's more than enough of those back here. Take it slow and I'll keep them coming." Red said.

"Where is he Red? I know you know."

"Olive? What's it going to take?"

Downing another third and chasing it with another mouthful of pretzels, "It's going to take," Olive said between chewing, "you telling me where he is!"

Opening another bottle, putting it in front of her and filling the bowl with fresh pretzels, Red ignored her hoping she would fill up on beer and pretzels and forget this foolishness.

"Give me change for the cigarette machine." Olive demanded.

"What's your brand?" Red asked opening the cigarette machine.

"Just toss me a pack. They all smoke the same."

Reaching in for a pack and locking the machine, Red smacked the top of the pack against the heel of his hand, unwrapped it and tapped it against the side of fingers working two cigarettes up through the opening. Olive took one. He took the other. With one match, he lit both and then tossing the burned match to the floor to sweep up later, he sat down on a stool beside Olive.

"Why?"

"She's sick."

Shaking his head at the obvious. Olive dug in.

"Yeah, I know. You've heard it before but this time it's different."

"Different how?"

Olive stared him down letting him fill in the blanks with his own imagination. She had caused enough trouble today and burned enough bridges. Red Connors had been more than good to her in years past. Supporting her when no one else would and keeping her affair with her sister's husband a secret. Keeping it so well at times she questioned herself whether he knew anything at all.

"Dying? She's dying?"

Olive remained quiet. She didn't say her sister was dying and if truth be told weren't they all dying? He was on the right track. Give him enough time and he would soon be feeling so guilty for keeping quiet he would be giving up everything he knew to ease his conscience.

"Chattanooga. Whenever he needs to get away. Especially since Marly passed. He heads to Chattanooga to Marly's sister's place. A boarding house. He stays there until. Well, until he thinks through whatever he has on his mind. I don't have to tell you, of all people, how the man is."

Red folded the cigarette on itself and lit another.

"Chattanooga? But how?"

"Train. He gets to Nashville. Don't ask me how. You can figure that one out just as well as anyone can. Catching the train to Chattanooga and well, I'd have to be a fortune teller to tell you what happens from there. All I know is he and Marly would go down there whenever she could pull the money together and Tinkum has kept going since her passing."

Olive finished both bottles of beer and licking her finger clean of the salt from the bowl. "Who else knows about this? About the regular trips to Chattanooga? About Marly's sister's place?"

"I can only assume the boys do. Ram. Henry. Arvis."

Olive sat quietly letting the information settle into her brain. Red mistook her silence and began to regret telling her. The last thing he wanted to do was hurt Olive. She was misunderstood. He didn't want to add to her misery.

"Why don't you give me a minute or two to sweep up and I'll drive you home?"

"Where's your broom? I'll help. It's the least I can do. You've helped me tonight Red." Olive fought back tears. "I appreciate it." Red studied the floor avoiding Olive's watery eyes. Only thing worse than seeing a woman cry is seeing a mean woman brought to tears. He just wasn't man enough to handle it.

Red nodded toward the corner where a broom and mop leaned.

Chapter Fourteen

Gus Poselinski sat quietly at the small kitchen table sipping coffee that was more cream than coffee. The dew was burning off the tree leaves outside the kitchen window making him wish he was doing anything but wasting yet another day on his lazy cousin. Tinkum had been in town less than six months and already he had Gus regretting running into him at the train station. But Gus knew better than to wish anything of the sort knowing that if Tinkum was in town he would find his way to the boarding house whether it was hitching a ride in his delivery truck like he did with the woman and boy or like he had many times before but never with someone with him.

Gus had given his cousin enough time, in his opinion, to come clean. Spill the beans. Cough up the story. What was he doing back in Chattanooga so soon from his last visit? And, who are the woman and boy. For almost six months since Tinkum approached Gus at the train station acting like he had never laid eyes on him before in his life. Gus had given his mother every opportunity to get the story. She was gifted that way. With running a boarding house for nearly thirty years, Betty Poselinski, Mrs. Posey to everyone but family, could weasel the smallest of details from a person without them even knowing they had uttered anything out of the ordinary. Never one to gossip, Betty believed it was her duty as innkeeper and upstanding citizen to know the people eating and sleeping under her roof whether they were there for one night like the man that claimed to be a member of the royal family of Denmark and was just passing through back in the fall of '25 or whether it was old man Whitaker that showed up one day with a suitcase full of lady's unmentionables, samples he called them, and practically moved in as a permanent resident, Betty knew more about them before their heads hit the pillow than their closet relative. How she did it, Gus really couldn't say. It appeared as nothing more than friendly conversation.

How do you do? What brings you to our neck of the woods? How long will we enjoy your company?

And before you know it, she knew all there was to know about a person. Betty said it was being a good hostess and being a good listener. For her, it came natural. For Gus, not so much.

And, Tinkum was living proof. If Gus couldn't get any further with someone he knew. Someone he was related to. How would he ever manage with someone he was meeting for the first time? Someone like Rose Lee and her son George.

"Morning Mr. Gus." George said sitting down at the kitchen table. His cowlick standing straight up from the center of his forehead. It looked as if the boy had slept face down all night giving no rest to the white lock of hair. His black eyebrows raised in question. His black eyelashes heavy with the remnants of sleep.

"What's got you up so early on a Saturday?" Gus asked tussling the boy's hair in a vain attempt to see if the cowlick would submit. It did not.

"Fishing." George answered looking around as if he had lost something or someone.

"Fishing sounds good. You and Tin...I mean Marly going fishing?" Gus choked.

"No sir. Mr. Whitaker is taking me."

"Whitaker?"

"Yes, sir."

Gus had never seen Whitaker do anything other than read. Read the newspaper until the print was too smudged for anyone else to read. Read the Reader's Digest until the pages were too creased. Or the Bible, something Gus wasn't too keen on reading.

Doubting the boy understood Whitaker's intentions. Expecting Whitaker was probably making a reference to something he had read about fishing. Maybe one of those Bible passages he was always quoting about fishing. Maybe he confused George. No wonder the boy looked like he slept on the top of his head, he had spent the night restless waiting for morning and his fishing adventure with Mr. Whitaker, the reader of all things adventurous.

Just as Gus was about to pour himself a tad more coffee to warm the cream in his cup, and just as he was about to explain to George that he must have misunderstood Mr. Whitaker and that if he still wanted to go fishing he would take him, the kitchen door swung open.

Standing in the space where the kitchen door had been was Eugene Whitaker in his three piece seersucker suit and his hat in his hand.

"Ready to go Georgie-boy?"

"Yes sir."

"Well, let's get to moving. Bus won't wait on us."

George jumped to his feet. His shoelaces falling untied.

"Wait a minute George. Let's get those laces good and tight before you head out." Gus said. Pulling the little boy onto his knee, Gus tied double knots in the boy's shoe laces. George's face beamed with excitement. It matched Whitaker's. Gus was full of doubt and suspicion. The old man and the boy were not dressed for fishing. Whitaker in his Sunday best and the boy in the short pants and shirt his mother brought in for him with her pay check from her job at the dry cleaners. She had been buying clothes with every pay check. Some little something for her. A blouse or stockings. Some little something for him. A shirt and new laces. His were always breaking.

Before letting the boy down from his knee, Gus asked, "You two are dressed awful fancy for fishing? You know the fish don't care what you wear. And, who takes the bus to go fishing anyways?" He teased the boy but his words were shot straight to Whitaker. And, they didn't miss their mark.

Whitaker bristled slightly then in his usual calm demeanor he explained without pretense that he was taking the boy to town to buy fishing gear. Something every boy, in his opinion, should possess. He started to suggest Gus was welcome to come along but stopped just short of offering the invitation.

George took Mr. Whitaker's hand and the two left the kitchen and Gus sitting staring at the swinging kitchen door.

"You two have fun. You sure you don't need me to come along? Alright then, see you later on. And George, you be good for Mr. Whitaker. Make your mother proud. Understand?"

Gus overheard Tinkum encouraging the twosome as he passed them on their way out the front door. He listened as Tinkum came nearer and he prepared himself to not look too interested in what had just taken place. Gus was more than curious but he knew his cousin well and if he expected to get any answers out of Tinkum Price it was going to have to be with care not force. Tinkum was as private as they came but he was also the only family Gus had besides his mother. And, as far as Gus knew, he and his mother were all the family Tinkum had.

"Morning!" Tinkum said pushing through the kitchen door. "Looks to be a good one."

Pouring coffee and making an effort to look out the kitchen windows and door.

"Sun is warming up fast. Going to be another hot one. And here we sit drinking coffee." Tinkum laughed. He felt the tension in the room and saw it on his cousin's face and riding up his broad shoulders. "Got something on your mind there, Gus?"

Gus knew better than to bite so quickly. He had paid the price one too many times with Tinkum's brand of curiosity. He knew his cousin wasn't asking out of concern. He was telling him not to be concerned.

"Nope. Can't say I do." Gus said over the brim of his cup.

"Thinking on going down to Nashville for a spell. Rose is busy with her job at the dry cleaners. She and George are settled in good here. Don't need me poking around under foot day in and day out."

Tinkum sipped on his coffee collecting his thoughts and waiting for his cousin to object. He always objected.

"Yeah, think I'll head on over to the station. Reckon I'll be back home by supper time if not sooner."

Tinkum emptied his cup. Poured another. And, still no objection. Gus sat stoic.

"Well, tell your mother I appreciate her putting me up these past few months. Not sure when I'll be back this way again. May not be before the first of the year as usual. Got to get on back and see how things are. Know things don't stay like you left them if you stay gone too long."

Tinkum drained the coffee from the cup in two swallows. Still no reaction from his cousin.

"Alright then." Placing the cup in the sink, Tinkum goaded his cousin one last time. "Don't reckon you'd mind dropping me off where you found me?"

Gus jumped to his feet sending his chair falling backwards to the floor and sending Tinkum into a fit of laughter. Gus, his fists clinched and his face contorted, was too blinded by his anger. Anger that had been building for nearly twenty years of going toe to toe with Tinkum. He didn't see or hear Tinkum laughing.

"You mean that rock you crawled out from under six months ago?" Gus said through gritted teeth.

Laughing to the point of being bent double, Tinkum tried to calm his cousin. "Whoa, take it easy. If you enjoy my company so much. Say so. I'll stay on a little longer. No need getting all worked up and kicking up a dust storm in your mama's kitchen. And, speaking of your mama..." Tinkum paused to gauge Gus's reaction to the sobering effect of mentioning his mother. Gus's face went pale. His shoulders fell limp and his clinched fists complied. "I don't think she would take too kindly to you busting up her chairs like that. You know what happened the last time you lost your temper. It'll be my guess you're still pulling splinters out of your backside from that one." Tinkum clapped his hands together to hold back his full onslaught of laughter bending double again.

"Well, speak of an angel and one will appear. Good morning Aunt Betty." Tinkum said looking past his cousin. His cousin that had lost all color in his face and stood frozen waiting for the sound of his mother's voice to rain judgment on him.

"What are you two doing down here? I heard the front door close then it sounded like someone slammed the back door. What's my chair doing on its back? Gus, put the chair right." Betty Poselinski spoke without looking at her son or nephew. She busied herself in the kitchen with her morning chores. Breakfast was light on Saturday mornings because so many slept in or made other plans. She offered coffee to those that wanted it and a tray of donuts she made the night before. No one ever complained about the day old pastry and in her opinion there was no need for complaining. It never changed anything for the better.

"We're just enjoying a cup of coffee and making plans for the day." Tinkum said with a smirk. He watched as Gus set the chair back up on its feet and then sat it on as quiet as a housecat.

"Well that's good. I know Rose is working today. Eugene and George were going to go to town. And the couple in four will be checking out in a couple of hours. They are on their way to Atlanta and just needed a place to sleep for the night. Down from Raleigh. He is in sales of some sort. And she has an aunt in Atlanta that she hasn't seen in a while. In the hospital there. In Atlanta. Wanted to get down there before it's too late. Suppose it's something serious."

Betty placed the donuts on the tray and filled the percolator with fresh coffee grounds and water.

"Betty Poselinski! Are you telling me you don't know no more than that with these two under your roof for more than twelve hours? Sales of sort. Hospital. You're slipping. Guess it was bound to happen sooner or later." Tinkum teased between bites of donut.

Betty blushed and laughed knowing her nephew meant no harm. She knew more about the young couple than she let on but if she told everything she knew every time she opened her mouth there would be nothing to keep her amused when there was no one around to tell anything to – besides what did her nephew and son care if she knew more about those two. They had enough they were trying to manage without trying to manage someone else's life.

Betty knew Tinkum was up to something showing up unannounced and with a woman and child in tow. A woman and child that he hardly knew if he knew at all. There was no way getting by Betty's watchful and skillful eye. She knew a snow job when she saw one. Tinkum may run fast and smooth with everyone else but she knew when he was up to something. And, there was no mistaking he was up to something with this woman and boy.

And, Gus had his own secrets. Running his delivery business. She knew he made runs in and out of the mountains. And she knew what went on deep in those hollows. But, she also knew ignorance is bliss if and when the government men came calling.

Chapter Fifteen

Gilford Taggart dozed to sleep with his hand resting on the pistol. The night was spent driving the distance from Nashville to Chattanooga. It had been a long time since he stayed awake all night. Four years to be exact. Four years since he sat in the waiting room of the hospital waiting for the doctor to tell him if it was a boy or girl. His pocket filled with cigars and no one to give them to – no one to join him in celebrating the birth of his child – no one but Rosalee. But Rosalee wasn't the cigar smoking type. Gilford wasn't either but it was tradition and he wasn't about to start breaking with tradition on this solemn occasion.

Church bells echoed off the mountain tops announcing the doors would be opening soon and services would commence. Gilford felt the cold dread of guilt snake its way up from its pit in his conscience reminding him in the voice of Sister Juliann that God's people did not avoid the communion of saints. It had been the good Sister's voice that governed his thinking and actions for most of his life. He wondered what she would say if she saw him now. If she knew the circumstances. The difficulty. The plans.

Shaking off the thoughts before they took root and changed his course of action, Gilford pushed himself up into the car seat and studied the map he bought at the truck stop. He had been to Chattanooga plenty of times on business. But this was a different sort of business and it demanded a certain attention to detail.

He knew he could just drive into town. Drive up to the dry cleaners. And, waltz in and confront Rosalee. He wanted to – he wanted to do just that. But he knew that would only make things worse. Sure he could convince her to come back to Nashville with him. He had that way with her. But that wasn't going to keep her in Nashville with him. She had to want to be there. That was the only way to insure she wasn't going to ever do something like this again.

Part of him wondered why. Why did she take off? Why did she choose this place of all places? And, how long had she been planning it? But, the other part of him. The part he listened to the most. The part that sounded like the stern yet gentle trill of Sister Julianne. Convinced him he didn't need answers to those questions because getting those answers wouldn't change the fact that she was here. Here in Chattanooga – on her own – with their son – and wasn't making any show of letting him know she had left their home in Nashville.

If George Gilford Taggart learned anything from being on the road selling feed and seed it was stick to what you know. And, what he knew right now was he needed to find his wife. One thing at time is what the Sister would advise. Master that one thing and then move on to the next.

Pulling out of the cover of the pine trees, Gilford drove down the mountain careful at each hairpin curve and inching slowly over every incline being unfamiliar with the roads and the terrain and feeling the swell of pride fill his chest to know he climbed the mountain in the predawn hours with no light other than the pale headlamps of the car.

***

Pressing her back against the pew, Rosalee Taggart took inventory. Her hair, nicely curled from the strips of cotton fabric Mrs. Posey gave her to roll her hair on, was clean and styled. A style she had seen on a recent customer at the dry cleaners. Her dress, a simple shirtwaist she purchased at the dress store around the corner from the dry cleaners, clean and pressed. Her stockings, straight and no runs. Her shoes, polished no scuffs. Her son, scrubbed clean including the scrapes on his knees from too many attempts to clear the boarding house front porch steps in one jump and landing on the sidewalk knees first. He smelled of soap and shoe polish. His laces perpetually slipping out of their knots. She leaned to tie them just as the organist played the first note of the invocation. The sanctuary filled with the sound of the pipe organ and the rustle of bodies in their starched Sunday best rising to stand.

As much as she hated herself for doing it, Rosalee's mind wondered from one thing to another throughout the church service. George's head pressed against her arm as he napped. She was thankful he was a good child and she didn't mind that he fell asleep in church. It was better than the alternative and she knew there would be plenty of Sundays in his future to sit awake and listen intently.

Her mind raced from Nashville to Chattanooga. From the dry cleaners to the boarding house. From Marly to Gilford. From Mrs. Posey to Eunice. Around and around she kept making the trip. Taking inventory still. This time not with her appearance but with her choices. She was being pulled in two different directions. She was torn on whether she had stayed long enough and it was time to go back. Or if she had outstayed her welcome and it was time to find another place to live. If she moved from the boarding house, where would she go? If she went back home to Nashville, what would be here reason for returning? Had she been gone long enough for things to change? She had completely forgotten what she needed to change in the first place. Was it her? Was it Gilford? She had gotten so busy trying to figure out what to do now that she was somewhere else. She had forgotten why she was there in the first place.

She knew she enjoyed working at the dry cleaners. Or at least she knew she enjoyed the company of the dry cleaners' owner Eunice. Very much like her sister Doris, Eunice was not one to hold back her opinion of things or people. And, Rosalee had found a new sense of freedom working so closely with the outspoken woman. She felt safe with Eunice. Something she had never felt while living in Nashville. Living with Gilford.

She knew she enjoyed the company of Mrs. Posey. She gave her a sense of family and the familiar. The routine of the boarding house was comforting and the safety she felt being there far out weighted the sleepless nights she had while living in their home in Nashville. Days and nights spent waiting on Gilford to return from work only to have him just as distant when he was at home as when he was away traveling for work.

Rosalee never knew how lonely for companionship she was until she was surrounded with so many people interested in how she was doing and showing interest in her and George. She missed Nashville. It had been her home for all of her twenty-three years. It had been where she met and married Gilford. It had been where they had their son. But in all of those twenty-three years, Rosalee could count on one hand the number of times she truly felt like she belonged. Something had always tugged at her heart. Pulled in a direction that was unknown to her until now. Until she took the first step of stepping out of her make-believe life and into a life she was building for herself and for her son. She had been living a life as flat and artificial as the paper dolls she played with as a girl.

Tears ran down her face. Silent and small. She wiped them from her chin just before they fell to her folded hands in her lap. Her white glove concealing a thin embroidered handkerchief. She dabbed the corners of her eyes and held the handkerchief to her nose. Its fragrance reminding her of the smell of home. The lavender sachets she kept in her dresser drawers. It was the small things that hurt the most. If she never laid eyes on George Gilford Taggart again she doubted she would shed a tear but the small things were enough to send her running back if for no other reason but to hold onto the memories of what could have been.

Mrs. Posey set the table. George marched behind her handing her folded linen napkins for each place setting. Sunday dinner had been warming in the oven since before church services. The boarders would be around the table soon.

"You're a good helper Georgie-boy. I think I'll keep you."

"Can't I'm already taken. But you can borrow me."

Mrs. Posey laughed at the boy's honesty and sincerity.

"George please go change your clothes before we sit down to eat. Mother can't take advantage of Miss Eunice's good nature forever and continue to bring your stained clothes in for cleaning."

Rosalee scolded gently. She appreciated her son's willingness to help and Mrs. Posey and Mr. Whitaker's willingness to entertain her son. She appreciated too Marly's willingness to father George when it wasn't his duty to do so. From the minute they met in the train station, Marly had been more attentive and fatherly than George's own father had been in the four years the child had been in the world. How complete strangers could be so understanding and giving would, it felt to Rosalee in the moment, forever escape her.

"He is a good helper and good company. You and Marly have done a good job Rose." Mrs. Posey complimented. She knew she was treading a thin line but the words were out before she had time to redirect them.

Rosalee blushed and regretted it. She had never blushed before when someone complimented her on the fine job she and Gilford had done. But then again, try as she might, standing there in the boarding house dining room beside a table set for twelve, in a town that was not her own, she could not remember a time when she and Gilford and George had been anywhere together where someone would observe them as a family and have an occasion to compliment her and Gilford on their fine parenting.

"Mrs. Posey Sunday dinner smells wonderful! Is that apple pie I'm smelling?" Lawrence Gruber from Memphis had checked in to his room last night after hours. A regular at the boarding house he had come to expect a full table on Sunday. And, he had come to expect delicious desserts.

"Mr. Gruber, I wouldn't disappoint you for all the gold in Fort Knox. Yes, that's apple pie you're smelling. Made fresh this morning and ready for your consumption after you've enjoyed the catfish I fried up from Mr. Whitaker and Georgie's first fishing trip." Mrs. Posey filled water glasses, coffee cups and tea glasses before leaving the sideboard.

"Fishing you don't say! Tell me Eugene, is there a secret to fishing for catfish?" Gruber asked passing the platter of fish.

Eugene Whitaker placed a filet on George's plate then placed two on his before passing the platter across in front of George to Marly. Marly laughed at the question and helped himself to two filets.

"Well it wouldn't be a secret for long, would it Georgie-boy..." Eugene Whitaker gently elbowed the boy while filling his plate with each passing bowl, "if we shared it."

Gruber laughed along with everyone else at the table. "You got a good point there."

"My guess is there's a difference between the fishing and the catching." Tinkum said adding his two cents to the lively exchange catching the last bit of the laughter before the bowls came to rest and heads were bowed for prayer.

Father Donovan stood to say grace. A Sunday regular, he was just as much at home at the head of the table at the boarding house as he was in the pulpit at St. Paul's Episcopal Church.

Forks scraped the bone china and ice rattled in glasses while conversation floated around the room keeping everyone at the table engaged and entertained. No one noticed the car sitting across the street. No one saw the man leaning against the car door smoking a cigar. No one knew he had followed slowly behind their small procession down the street from St. Paul's on the corner to the opposite corner of the block at the boarding house. A busy street on any given day with cars passing. No one paid any particular attention to the Buick with Nashville license plate.

Chapter Sixteen

Fletcher Pittman had held his piece as long as he could. Most would say he had lost his mind. Not because he was racing to his daughter's house to put an end to her husband's rambling ways. But because he decided to wait as long as he had. It was Fletcher's nature to fight first and ask questions later. A perfect blend of Hessian and Ulster Irish flowed through his veins keeping his hands balled up in fists and his back braced for battle. It suited Fletcher. Built like a tree. The man stood every inch of six foot three. And weighted every pound it took to support his massive frame. The only thing passive about Fletcher was his low voice often confused for softness.

Anger and confusion had festered inside of Fletcher until he couldn't take it any longer. He warned Tinkum the last time he took to the road and left Bea standing on the porch crying and begging him to come back. Fletcher's porch of all places. Couldn't wait until he got home to decide to take to the road. Fletcher would have maybe given him the benefit of the doubt. Any man would have trouble with an ailing woman. Fletcher knows if Bea wasn't his own flesh and blood he would be like everyone else on the ridge and wonder just how any sane person could handle such sickness. But, Bea was his flesh and blood. And, she was under his roof right up to her last birthday. He had heard her utter her first words. Take her first steps. And bloom into a woman. All under his roof. All under his watchful eye.

Most days he regretted ever giving Tinkum Price a job as a laborer on his farm. An extra set of hands was needed and the two sets of soft female hands just wasn't comparable to a man's hands. Setting Tinkum to the plow saved Fletcher from the poor house but it cost him more than he was willing to pay.

The pickup truck fishtailed around the hairpin curves of the ridge and sailed down the slopes. Fletcher almost missed his turnoff down in to Mud Flats because he was going so fast and because he was so angry. His wrestled the steering wheel into submission as he whipped the truck to the right and caught the outside edge of the gravel road nearly sending the truck spinning.

Cussing under his breath and blaming Tinkum for everything under the sun, Fletcher didn't see Dr. Bass's car pass. He didn't see the doctor swerve to miss being bowled over. He didn't see the doctor waving to get Fletcher's attention just before his car slid off the road and into the ditch. It would be days before gossip circulated through its regular channels and gets around to Fletcher Pittman that he ran the good doctor off the road in one of his angry tares. By the time the word circles its way up the ridge and back down, by the time it's been whispered by every tongue, by the time it makes its way to Fletcher Pittman's ears, he will have forgotten what sparked his anger to put him behind the wheel of his pickup and send him racing over to Bea's house. But his gristmill of anger never stops it only slows.

"Pap! What in the world are you doing ramming that truck up in the yard like that? Look at the damage on the front end. It's got brakes don't it?"

The sound of wood cracking and metal folding sent Olive Pittman running out onto her sister's rickety front porch to see what had happened. The rare chance of an automobile passing by sent heads turning in the general direction of the road to see who or what was passing by. No one came down the hollow's gravel road without purpose. Mud Flats was not on the scenic route for anyone in Jessup County. Narrow gravel roads barely accommodating one vehicle much less two trying to pass pitched at odd angles along the northeast side of the ridge. No one came through this way unless they had business with one of the few residents or was on their way to the cemetery that rested at the bottom of the hollow.

"Brakes work just fine. Never you mind about the brakes. Where's Tinkum?" Fletcher said. His words landing hard at Olive's feet. She feared Fletcher's reaction to her disrespect. Months spent out from under her father's grip made her forget who she was in his eyes. She knew she was not responsible for Tinkum leaving. Not this time. But she couldn't help feeling guilty for playing a part in her sister's misery.

Olive knew no one but Red Connors knew about her relationship with Tinkum. It was a secret. There were times she wondered if anything happened at all or if she imagined it or dreamed it. Either way, the guilt was there and it was real. And, whatever came after guilt was now making her get bowed up at the slightest thing and step willfully into the crosshairs of her father's wrath. Something she had never done.

Dropping her head and her tone Olive answered, "Tinkum's not here. Hasn't been."

"You're telling me he hasn't been back in all this time!"

Olive was shocked at her father's sudden concern for Tinkum's whereabouts. Where had Fletcher been this whole time she wondered. Was he not keeping up with what was going on over here? Did he not consider if she had not come back to his house, to her childhood home, to her long list of chores and responsibilities that maybe, just maybe it was because there had not been that first sign of Tinkum Price.

"I reckon I stopped looking for him some time ago." Olive said with emotion. More emotion than she was aware had been on the surface ready to leap from her heart and free itself from its constraints. Was she safe speaking so freely to her father? Would he hear the longing in her voice? Would he see the misery on her face?

Fletcher spit a stream of caramel colored tobacco juice from his crusted lips. "Can't say I wouldn't have done the same thing."

Olive felt the air return to her lungs and her shoulders roll back into place. Fletcher was comforting her as best he could. He was losing his head of steam. And, it was because of her. Because she needed him this time. Not Beatrix.

"You've done a fine thing staying over here taking care of her." Fletcher nodded toward the house acknowledging the place his sickly daughter lay. Beatrix strained to hear all that was being said on the other side of the screened door. If the wind had been blowing she could have heard it all but there was no wind today and all she could hear was Fletcher's voice keeping time with Olive's. The words fell long before they made their way to her bedside.

"Can't say I put too much thought into any of it. Just did what I thought was right." Olive said. She was testing the waters. She knew if she baited her hook too much Fletcher would do one of two things. Get angry and leave. Or turn the tables and find fault in her. Either way, she would lose. She had no idea what sent him over the ridge in a ball of fire and her curiosity was eating a hole in her brain. A little sugar on the hook never hurt anyone.

Fletcher nodded in agreement with his daughter. Kicking at the ground trying to remember just what got him stirred up and trying to gain some momentum to finish his errand of righting a wrong he studied the ground until his words came to him. Olive knew to wait. It was instinctive.

Neither one saw or heard Beatrix until she was on the porch. Standing in her cotton gown. Her round belly pulling the gathers to the left and right. She held onto the porch post for support.

"Y'all going to stand out here all day and jowl or are you going to come inside?"

Beatrix tried to sound hospitable but instead she sounded insulted. The looks on her father's face and her sister's matched the shame she felt for daring such a risky move.

Rushing to her side, Fletcher took her left arm and Olive her right in spite of the fact she didn't need or want their assistance and helped her back into the house and into the bed.

"Pap you didn't need to come all the way over here. You could have called." Beatrix said winded from the short walk to and from the porch.

Olive and Beatrix stared at their silent father waiting for him to explain why he was there when he could have easily picked up the telephone. They both knew he didn't like the contraption but if he was determined to know how things were going it would have been the easiest way to find out.

Fletcher Pittman didn't know where to begin. He knew there were too many facts about what sent him racing over to his daughters that he could share with them. Things a daughter just didn't need to know about their father. Things he didn't care to admit to himself. But he had information. Information he had gotten from a source that he knew would upset his daughters if they knew. Besides it was his business who he kept time with and being a widower for all their lives, he needed companionship that they would never understand. It was too late now to explain his relationship with Gertie Margolus. It wasn't no one's business but his and Gertie's.

It was Gertie that had shared with him that Tinkum had taken off to Chattanooga. How she knew escapes Fletcher now as he remembers his evening with the young gypsy. He was too quick to get lost in her ebony eyes and raven hair. Fletcher felt like he was sawed in half staring into their young fresh faces full of innocence and thinking about the woman he shared a secret life with – a woman that was not their mother.

Clearing his throat and deciding to take a different approach than what he first took, Fletcher sat down and tried his best to appear like he was just coming to visit. To check on Bea. Hear what the doctor had to say on his last visit. See how they were holding up for supplies. Groceries. Gas for Olive's car or the tractor. Ask if they needed him to take care of anything before he headed back home to feed and milk.

But all the while Olive knew better. She knew there was more to his visit than he was letting on. She was the one that stepped out on to the porch after he rammed his truck to a stop in the tree. She knew he was upset more so than usual when he got out of the truck and it had nothing to do with the truck or the tree. She sat patiently as Beatrix told him about the doctor just being there minutes before he came up. How the doctor said she was doing fine and that she just needed to stay in bed and keep resting and the baby would be just fine. Olive watched as Beatrix blushed red and Fletcher did too both for different reasons that only Olive could wonder and guess about. She assumed Beatrix was embarrassed that she walked out onto the porch only after being told how great things were going because she was staying put. How that must have looked and sounded to her father the master rule keeper for her to flaunt her good health however fleeting. She could only assume Fletcher was embarrassed to hear about the delicate details however few they were of a woman's health even though the woman was his daughter. Olive could only sit and wonder about all that was being said and playing out in front of her. An afternoon of pretending she hadn't planned on.

A billowy cloud of silence settled in between them. Resting in its ease, they each took a moment to replay the visit. Suddenly Fletcher sprang from the ladder back chair he had been sitting in as if stung by a bee or inspiration, and walked toward the door. "I need to be heading back. You take care Bea and do as the doctor says." He said to his daughter in bed without looking back over his shoulder. She tried to smile believing it was said with tender loving care but it sounded more like an excuse to leave her company.

Olive jumped up more as a reaction to the sudden movement than anything else and followed her father outside. She wanted to say be careful or see you later or some such parting words but it all sounded like nonsense in her head and knew it would sound stupid if she said it. Fletcher rescued her from her conflict by motioning for her to come to the truck door. With the truck idling to mask the sound of his voice he felt confident he could speak without being heard by the well trained ear of his daughter inside the house.

"You need to get yourself to Chattanooga." Fletcher said.

Olive waited for him to explain and when no explanation followed she asked the obvious.

"Why? What's in Chattanooga?"

"Not what. Who. Stop by the house. I'll give you money for the trip. Don't worry her about it. Tell her whatever you need to tell her. Tell her I came here to check on her and get you to come home to help me get the jars ready for canning. I'm expecting we'll put up quite a bit this year and no need waiting to the last minute to see what we're going to need. That's close enough to the truth that she won't question it or worry about what is going on." Fletcher paused and pulled a piece of scrap paper from his bib pocket. "Take this. You'll need it. It's the address. Find him and get him home. If for no other reason but to see his child once he's born. After that if he wants to take off, well, that's on him. But no man needs to walk this earth not ever seeing his child. No man."

Olive's knees grew weak. Fletcher was unloading more on her than she believed she was capable of understanding or doing. She knew he saw himself in her. She knew he saw his late wife, their mother, in Beatrix. She knew that's why he was so hard on her and so gentle on her twin sister. But, there was more being said or not said more between the lines of what Fletcher was saying than she was quick enough to understand.

She didn't have time to figure it out right now. He had given her a job to do and she didn't have the right to refuse. She took the scrap of paper and held it still folded in her hand until he was long out of sight up the gravel road. She stood next to the tree with his gutted bark and watched the blanket of gravel dust settle back down onto the road. Too afraid to open the paper and read what was written on it, she instead slipped it into the glove compartment of her car and went back inside to lie to her sister.

Chapter Seventeen

Olive pulled the Buick up to the pump and waited for the attendant to come out from the garage bay and fill her gas tank. She hated waiting. Waiting on anyone. But she really hated waiting on a man. Drumming her fingers on the steering wheel she watched as he sauntered across the parking lot to the pump. Unhitched the pump handle and began pumping gas with no thought to ask her just what she needed or wanted. Working his way around to the front of the car, she peered through the space between the opened hood and the dashboard. She watched as he pulled the dip stick out, wiped it on the pink shop rag, and put it back into the engine. Wiping his hands on his coveralls, he slammed the hood and returned to the gas pump. All of this done without a glance or word in Olive's direction. She had never felt more invisible. Her pride tempted her to pull away without paying. It would serve him right. But, she knew she wouldn't get far before the law, or worse, Fletcher, was catching up with her. Hauling her back. Back to the service station. Back to the rude attendant. Back to her invisibility. It just wasn't worth it.

"That'll be a buck and a quarter."

Olive dug through her pants pocket for the last five she had. She could feel the attendant's eyes on her. He disapproved of women wearing pants. She knew the look. She saw it on every man's face. Every man but Tinkum. He liked her fiery temperament and the way her hind-end filled out the seat of her pants.

Holding the five in his hand as if he had never seen one, the attendant said, "If you're going far, you're going to need a quart. Fletcher know you're burning oil?"

Olive knew he was trying to sell her oil but what burned her more than her engine burning oil was this idiot assuming she had to check with her daddy before buying a quart of oil.

"Fletcher? I don't know what my daddy has to do with m-y car burning oil. If you've got a quart to sell then sell me one. If you'd rather check with my daddy first, then you can sell him one but it won't be for this car."

Laughing to himself and galling Olive with every rise and fall of his shoulders, he said, "I couldn't place you at first. Well, I knew you were either Olive or Beatrix but after you opened your mouth there was no doubt which one you are. You're the hellion."

Olive should have not been bothered. She had been compared to Bea her whole life from family to friends to church members to classmates. Everyone felt the need to make distinctions between her and her identical twin sister. Couldn't tell them apart standing side by side but the minute they opened their mouth, everyone knew the sweet one, Beatrix, from the sour one, Olive.

"Hellion? You ain't seen hell yet. Give me my change and back out of the way unless you don't need those planks at the end of your legs you're trying to pass as feet." Charging the engine and dropping the gear shift down into first gear, Olive refused to reach out to take the change but let it drop through the window as she gunned the car and left the attendant standing staring.

Grumbling to herself. Blind with rage and wishing she was anywhere but on the ridge, Olive swerved to miss the slow moving tractor sending her Buick into the deep ditch.

"Arvis Ange! What in the world are you doing running the roads on that contraption! Look! Just look at my car! It's not enough the dang thing is burning oil. I guess the whole dang block is cracked now the way I hit that ditch! Don't just sit up there gawking! Get down here and help me! I've got places to go!" Olive spit and kicked pulling herself up out of the car wedged in the ditch.

Arvis wanted to laugh but knew better. From the looks of things, the car was in worse shape than Olive. If her mouth was working. And, God in His heaven and everything under it knew there was nothing wrong with her mouth. It was working just fine. If her mouth was working, chances are she was just fine too.

"If I've said it once, I've said it a hundred times. Someone was going to find themselves in a ditch. Just mark my words. The way they run these roads like they're stretched out flat instead of hairpin turns and hills that make your stomach drop out of ye quicker than the loop-to-loop at the fair. Yep, if I've said it once. I just knew it was a matter of time." Arvis spoke to himself watching as Olive climbed out of her car.

"What are you going on about? Can't you see I need help? Didn't you hear me say I've got places to be?" Olive tugged at her pants legs and worked her heel back into her shoe.

"I reckon we've all got places to be." Looking at Olive and then over at his tractor and back, "I reckon I could give you a ride." Arvis studied Olive then this tractor.

"I'm not getting on that thing..."Olive stopped short of finishing her thought. She knew better than to insult the man too deeply because he could climb back on his tractor and leave her standing on the side of the road for someone else to find. Whether she finished her thought out loud or not. She was determined she wasn't going to get on that tractor with Arvis.

Distracted suddenly by his pocket watch, Arvis moved toward his tractor with no apparent thought to helping Olive. She wasn't going to beg and she wasn't going to suggest to the man how to be a gentleman. Her pride was bruised beyond repair and she would rather stand right where she stood and wait for the rapture before she schooled Arvis Ange.

Just beyond the hill, a car engine was rising and falling with each dip and turn coming closer to where the tractor idled and Olive stood. Looking toward the hill expecting to see the car's front end rounding the bend just any second, Olive ignored Arvis. Arvis obliged her and did the same. Both were too absorbed in their own plans. Plans that were being delayed by the other.

"My lands! Olive Ann! What in the world happened? Are you alright?" Goldalena Filbry shouted across her car through the open windows. The music on the radio drifting out. Olive recognized the song. It was one of Tinkum's favorites. It was the one he played over and over on the jukebox at the Red Stagg. He spent a whole dollar the last time. Her feet barely touching the dance floor from being pulled up so close and tight to him. The look on Goldie's face turned Olive's stomach. The woman had the gift for looking through you and seeing your secrets. Their eyes locked on each other. Olive lost in thought dancing around the tavern in Tinkum's arms. Goldie seeing the scene but not seeing it all at the same time. She reached out and with two fingers turned the radio knob drowning the music and Olive's memory.

Brushing invisible dust from her knees and smoothing her hair, Olive stacked every vertebrae and said, "I'm fine." Glaring toward Arvis climbing into the tractor seat.

"Well, looks like you need a ride and a tow. I can get you where you need to go and we can call Bishop for a tow." Goldie motioned for Olive to get into her car.

Olive opened the car door still glaring up at Arvis but he wasn't paying her or Goldie any attention too lost in thought to care what either woman was saying or thinking about him.

Goosing the gas on the tractor, a cloud of smoke coughing up out of its exhaust pipe, Arvis grinded the gears sending the tractor jerking forward and slowly up the road. Goldie and Olive followed behind with little choice but to give the man and his tractor the right of way until he got where he was going or the road opened up for Goldie to pass safely.

Riding in silence, both watching with more curiosity than either were willing to admit, Goldie and Olive craned their necks to the right to see what they already knew. Arvis was on his way to the Gentry's. Taking a sharp right into the long gravel driveway that snaked up to the house on the hill, Arvis eased his tractor up alongside the clapboard house and was climbing down by the time Goldie and Olive passed by.

"Poor thing. I can't remember ever hearing of a body taking ill as fast as she has." Goldie said turning the knob on the radio until it clicked cancelling any sound from the radio.

"What'd they say it is?" Olive asked looking out the window. She wanted to sound interested. Concerned. Involved. But she wasn't. She never liked Caroline Gentry. If she was sick, she well deserved it. Too many times she made fun of Beatrix. Too many times she talked about Beatrix. Too many times she looked down her nose at Beatrix. At Olive. As far as Olive Pittman was concerned the world would be better off without Caroline Gentry.

"Don't matter what they say it is. She has given up. Given up on living. Can't expect to get better from anything once you're in that state of mind." Goldie said.

Olive tried to mask her shock. Was she really hearing this right? Caroline Gentry was so upset over something that she got sick and refuses to get well? For a half of a second, Olive felt sorry for Arvis. But by the time she realized it, it was gone.

"Well, I've never heard of such a thing. You're saying she has decided not to get well. That's just ridiculous. Arvis will get in there. He'll convince her." Olive said sounding more caring that she truly was.

"I don't know if Arvis can do anything about it. She has lost heart. It's that simple and that complicated." Goldie knew her words hit their mark when she saw the realization spread across Olive's face.

Adjusting in the seat, Olive stared out the window as if the answers to her own breaking heart was somewhere in the wooded ravines and bare bluffs of Scots Ridge. She knew the minute the words left her mouth she had gone too far at the barn. She knew it. Arvis knew it. Goldie knew it. Caroline was the only one that didn't know it. Not the way they did.

Arvis and Goldie and Olive knew the truth. Caroline only thought she did. And now, she lay dying drowning in a sea of misunderstandings and fever pitched deceit. In the end, Diphtheria will be in the doctor's chicken scratch on the death certificate but it will be whispered for years to come, she died of a broken heart.

Chapter Eighteen

Goldalena Filbry sat in her car trying her best to put as much distances between her ears and the argument inside the house. She had heard for years the Pittman twins were opposites in every way but she was beginning to wonder as she listened to their knock-down-drag-out if she had stumbled upon the one thing they had in common. Other than Tinkum Price.

"I just don't see what's got you all stirred up Olive? I asked a simple question and you 'bout bit my head off." Bea's voice cracked with emotion

"Get back in the bed! How many times do you have to be told! Seriously, how hard is it to stay in the bed! What I'd give for one day to lay about and have everyone else tote and fetch for me. Girl you don't know how good you've got it." Olive said between the sound of cabinet doors banging closed and pots and pans rattling.

"How good I've got it! You think being tied to this bed is so great. That just shows how little you really know. And, the last time I looked no one was begging you stay on here. Tinkum will be back any day and when he does..." Beatrix paused.

Goldie strained her ears to hear what was going on. The silence was more deafening than the screaming.

"What have you done now!" Olive screamed.

Goldie reached for the car door handle. She was just about ready to go inside to see what was going on and what if anything she could do to help when the cat fight resumed.

"I've had it. Do you hear me! I've had it Beatrix! You can lay there in the floor and die for all I care. It'll just be one more thing to blame me for anyway. What's one more dead woman on my hands!" Olive said panting. In spite of her comments, she was helping her sister back in the bed from where she slumped over a chair for support. The arguing had taken all the energy Beatrix had stored up and she was spent before trying to get back to bed.

"You didn't kill her Ollie. You know you didn't. I don't care what Daddy says." Bea said. Her voice had lost its shrill and was more compassionate.

"Daddy. You can call him what you want but Fletcher Pittman has never been a daddy to me. You know as well as I do that he blamed me the moment I took my first breath and she took her last. You know he believes I killed her. He'd have a wife and you'd have a mother if it hadn't been for me. And now," Olive stopped short of finishing her thought when she caught a glimpse of Goldalena Filbry sitting in her car waiting for her.

Olive had forgotten Goldie drove her home from her car in the ditch to call Elrod Bishop to come tow her out. The whole exchange with Arvis and then hearing about Caroline being sick and on her death bed had rattled her beyond anything had in a long time and then to come home and see Beatrix up cleaning the house. A mop bucket and mop at the ready and bed stripped of the bed clothes with the water filling in the washing machine outside was about all Olive could take. If she had one more woman, her sister or Caroline Gentry, die on account of her, it would send her over the edge. She just knew it.

"What are you talking about Olive. Who do you know that's dying?" Beatrix asked with a sincerity that changed the direction of Olive's heart and mind.

"No one. No one is dying. I was just being silly. Here, you go on in there and lay down on my bed. I'll get things finished around her and take care of this mess I've got my car in. No need for you to concern yourself with any of it."

Goldie missed most of the last part of the sisters' conversation as they moved further from the front of the house. Still feeling as though it would be best to stay put she waited for Olive to return to her instead of getting out of the car and venturing inside.

"You sure you don't mind driving me back down to my car?" Olive asked stepping down off the rickety front porch and crossing the small overgrown front yard.

Goldie bit her tongue to keep from speaking the obvious. It wasn't for her health that she sat there in the afternoon summer heat waiting for Olive to remember what it was that sent her inside. Of course she didn't mind finishing her errand. However well-intentioned it was Goldie was ready to be done with these two for a while. She was more than ready for Olive to get in the car so that she could drop her off and be done with her.

"No. Come on. I'll get you back down there and wait until Bishop comes along. You called him, right?" Goldie asked almost hating herself for asking but she had to know Olive remembered to call the mechanic. The last thing she wanted was to lock horns with Olive. Whatever had her riled up had nothing to do with Goldie Filbry. And, Goldie was glad for it.

Getting in the car as calm and collected as if they were on their way to a Sunday school social, Olive said, "Yeah, he's on his way."

"Reckon Arvis could help too if he is still in the area. Didn't think to just drive up to Caroline's and ask him to come pull you out." Once again, Goldie wanted to bite her tongue in two for saying what was on her mind instead of keeping her mouth shut. She didn't bit more believe it would have been a good idea to ask Arvis to help now than she did when she saw the car go off into the ditch and the tractor with its distracted driver stay on its course. She knew Arvis had Caroline on his mind and never knew Olive ended up in the ditch. He was so distracted by Caroline's illness and the guilt he feels for bringing it on that he wouldn't know it if a snow storm came up in the middle of summer.

Goldie knew it was stupid to mention Arvis and Caroline but her curiosity got the best of her and she wanted to see Olive squirm a bit. But squirm she did not. Instead Olive sat quiet lost in her own thoughts that she didn't hear a word Goldie said.

Not wanting to tempt fate too much, Goldie left well enough alone. She knew if she wanted to get information she could always pay Beatrix a visit. And, since she knew Olive was going to be busy with getting the car towed and its repairs, it would only be neighborly to check in on Beatrix while she was on the ridge.

Elrod Bishop blocked the road in both directions with his wrecker. Goldie pulled up as close as she could without getting in the mechanic's way. Olive jumped out of the car as soon as it came to a rolling stop.

"What do you think? Can you pull her out?" Olive asked knowing the answer but asked anyway.

Elrod ignored her and kept working.

Feeling bruised by the eldest Bishop's rudeness, Olive decided to leave him to his work and walk up to meet Arvis on his tractor. Halfway down the Gentry's long gravel driveway, Arvis slowed the tractor but kept it running closing the space between Olive coming up the driveway and him on the tractor heading towards the wrecker.

Chapter Nineteen

Goldie knew the moment she pulled back into the half-moon driveway of the house Tinkum Price shared with his wife and sister-in-law that guilt and shame would cover her like the cloud of road dust covered her car. It hadn't been a solid hour since she was parked in the same dirt patch with its smattering of gravel eavesdropping on Beatrix Price and her twin sister Olive Pittman going at it like a couple of stray cats. Goldie's curiosity was matched by her concern for the women. She had heard the rumors just like everyone else on the ridge, in Fulton and Tillman too about how Fletcher Pittman worked Olive like a man in the fields and how he kept Beatrix up on a shelf. Goldie knew it was no wonder Olive was as hard as stone and Beatrix as fragile as a feather. You didn't have to look past their daddy to know the source. But, Goldie, like everyone else in Jessup County knew too that Fletcher didn't ask for the hand that had been dealt him. No one deserved the misery that was heaped upon him. Barely married he lost his bride, Alice, in childbirth. Rumor spread like wildfire from the few that were present to witness it firsthand. Goldie trusted the source and knew it was as close to the truth as she could get without being there herself. Rumor had it that the minute Olive took her first breath Alice took her last. Fletcher was distracted by the news he had a daughter to hear he had two. Within the span of a heartbeat, his joy turned to sorrow when holding his newborn daughters he was told his wife had passed over to her reward. The rumor splits at this part and some say Fletcher placed the babies on either side of Alice and wept like a baby himself at her feet begging God to bring her back. Other say he handed the babies off to the gypsy midwife, Gertie, walked out the back door and fell upon his face in the backyard bargaining with God. Goldie believes the truth lies somewhere in between and as far as she is concerned the fine details aren't that important. He lost Alice. He lost hope. And, he lost heart.

Goldie knew for a fact that many of the women in the community tried their best to intervene and help Fletcher raise the girls but he wouldn't have none of it. Henry said one time in passing when the conversation of Fletcher Pittman had reached a point of turning friend on friend and ruining an otherwise perfect Sunday school social or fish fry, that the biggest mistake

Fletcher Pittman ever made was blaming his daughters for Alice's death. To this day Goldie can't remember anyone disagreeing with Henry about that and maybe it was because it was so obvious to everyone hearing it or maybe it was like so many other things that come from Henry Filbry, no one ever thought to disagree.

Right or wrong, Fletcher Pittman did blame the twins for Alice's death. And, he made them both pay. Olive lost any softness she would ever have behind a plow and mule. And, Beatrix lost any strength she would ever have shut up in the house.

Fletcher may have ruined them for happiness, his and theirs, but he couldn't undo what God had created. Splitting them right down the middle in equal parts long before they left their mother's womb, Olive and Beatrix Pittman, were equal halves of the same person. And, to Fletcher's greatest shame and constant reminder, they were not only identical versions of each other, they were identical version of Alice Pittman.

Goldie sat in the car debating on whether or not to go inside. She knew when she drove off earlier that Olive was fuming and fit to be tied. She could only imagine the shape Bea was in after tangling with her sister. Olive was carrying a heavy load. Goldie felt in her bones there was something dreadfully wrong with Olive and time would tell. She knew she had it in for Arvis Ange. Arvis had poked her one too many times and the stunt at the barn was only part of it. Goldie could see Olive was stewing on something when they passed the Gentry's. If Olive felt responsible for Caroline's illness, it wouldn't be surprising.

Goldie only heard bits and pieces from the cat fight between Bea and Olive. Distracted by Olive's uneasiness and playing it off as being concerned about the trouble she was having with the car in the ditch, Goldie was caught off guard when the two sisters tore into one another. Verbal jabs and screaming and crying poured out the screen door in sharp riffs separated by moment of silence heavy with emotional energy.

"You getting out and coming in?" Beatrix called from the bed. Her back ached low and deep. She rolled from side to side trying to find comfort and relief. She had seen the Buick when it passed the bedroom window with its perfect angle to the hilltop of the hollow. Anything coming in or out of the hollow had to pass the plane of that window and Beatrix being forced into bed rest didn't miss anything or anyone coming or going out of Mud Flats.

Goldie eased the screen door closed behind her and forced her shoulders to drop and release the tension that had been building.

"Realized earlier that it had been while since I stopped by to say howdy and see how you and the baby are doing. Figured since I was up here I'd stop back by before heading down the ridge."

Pushing herself up on her pillows and elbows, Beatrix asked, "Think you might be able to help me get these pillows situated? I can't get any comfort. I don't know what I've done to my back. Guess it's all this time laying up in this bed instead of moving about like a normal person."

Goldie tugged and pulled and fluffed and beat the pillows into submission. She wasn't sure if she did anything different than what they were before she tried but at least she made a big show of it.

"I wouldn't know anything about how anyone else would manage what you're dealing with Bea and maybe that's the key to getting through it is to take it a day at time and not look to how someone else is managing their day to day." Goldie said looking out the bedroom window at Milly hanging clothes on the line. Her round belly a constant hindrance to her daily chores. Four baby girls barely weaned and she is expecting again. If anyone needed a good talking to it would be Ram Hatch. But as far as Goldie knew, no one was making any headway in that direction.

"How does she do it? Them two oldest ones of hers are hellions on a good day and then she's got the twins." Beatrix laughed thinking about life with twins. "And, now. Now she's expecting again. Maybe this time it will be a boy and Ram will leave her alone for a while. At least a year or two." Beatrix laughed again. This time at her own joke.

Goldie laughed too but for different reasons. They all found it easy to discuss having and raising a family and maybe because she and Henry never said too much about it in front of anyone no one ever paid too much attention to how difficult it was for Goldie to see the wives of their friends round with motherhood year after year and she and Henry knowing without a doubt they'd never know the joy of having their own. No, people are too short sighted. Seeing the world only as it spins in their direction.

Changing the subject because the last thing Goldie had in mind this afternoon was gossiping, "When was the last time the doctor was here? Did you mention your back pain to him then?" She asked with sincerity. She needed to pull Bea's attention back into the room. And, she was somewhat concerned for Bea's back. Milly was known for having only back labor and if that's what this was Goldie didn't need to leave Beatrix alone and without medical attention.

Pushing herself upon the pillows higher, Bea thought for a moment then said, "Reckon it has been long enough. I guess he'll be by here in a day or two. Seems like just when I get to missing him he shows up." She exhaled with a deep sigh. "If only that worked for someone else."

Goldie knew Beatrix was talking about Tinkum and she made no bones about acknowledging it.

"When was the last time you saw Romeo?" Goldie teased.

"Yeah, he's a Romeo for sure." Beatrix laughed thinking somehow that was a compliment to her. "I wish I could say when was the last time I laid eyes on the man. Wish I could say when I expect to see him again. But, I'm telling you. The more time that separates us and the more I suspect he has found something or someone to keep him from finding his way back home, I begin to doubt I'll ever lay eyes on him again." Beatrix rubbed her belly. "It'll just be me and this little'un."

Goldie didn't know whether she wanted to laugh or cry. Beatrix was so sweet and stupid all at the same time and it was getting the best of Goldie. If Tinkum Price was anything, he was consistent. Goldie didn't know when he would return but she knew as well as she knew her own husband that he would be coming back. He always had and he always would.

"Well, I reckon you just need to rest like the doctor said and give things the time they need. This here baby will be here before you know it and you'll have more to do and more to keep you busy that you won't be worrying or wondering about Tinkum Price."

Still rubbing her belly absentmindedly, "Been thinking on Mama too. I know Olive don't like hearing it and Lord knows I can't say anything to Pap about it. And, with Tinkum gone, I can't tell him. But she sure has been on my mind hard and heavy. Olive gets so riled up anytime I mention it. I woke up this morning thinking on her and made the mistake of saying something. Guess that set the course for Olive because she has been fit to be tied all day. Just a few minutes ago, when y'all came through here, she was so wound tight I thought for sure she was going to..."

Goldie interrupted concerned Bea would get lost down one of her rabbit holes and lose train of thought. "Can't say you mentioning your mama this morning could have her riled up all day, do you?"

Beatrix studied on it and said, "You know now that you mention it, I think she was worked up about something else. Because, now that I think on it a bit, she never said anything this morning when I mentioned dreaming about Mama again. That's what I do. Have done it for years but it has gotten worse since the baby. She never said anything. I halfway expected it to because well, that's what she does but you know, she didn't. She went to bed mad about something or someone and you know what they say. She was still just as mad if not madder when she got up. I kinda feel sorry for whatever or whoever it is because for all you might have overheard earlier, I'm telling you now, that pales in comparison to what Olive is going to say or do when she finally decides who or what she is mad at."

Chapter Twenty

Tinkum had walked all night. The horizon was turning pink and he knew if he didn't make a decision soon he would be out of time and out of options. He hadn't planned on leaving. He never planned anything. Stirred by emotions and driven by impulse, he rarely knew what he was doing or where he was going until he was head long into a new scheme and half way through to the other side. Tonight was no exception.

A train whistle caught his attention and begged him to come. A siren of steel it sang its song of lonesomeness. A tune Tinkum knew all too well. Train cars slammed into one another. Back and forth they rolled in their slow dance. As if being moved by the hand of God, no one could be seen throughout the railyard. Tempted to sit on the grassy slope and watch for a while, Tinkum decided against it not wanting to deal with wet britches from the dew soaked ground. And before that thought could meander its way through his mind, cutting a path for the next temptation, he was overcome by the urge to hop onboard.

You gotta see her. Here's your chance. Jump on!

Before he knew what was happening, Tinkum was running alongside the moving train cars in one minute and in the next was trying to catch his breath laying waist deep inside a boxcar. Drawing his knees to his chest, he lay on his side for several minutes steading his breathing and letting his eyes adjust to the darkness. A smattering of straw and what he hoped was mud but he doubted it from the stench that was roiling off of it covered the rumbling floor of the boxcar. He felt he wasn't alone. Although he couldn't see anything he felt the presence of something. Something living, breathing, and watching. If it was cow dung and not mud, chances were there was a cow or two in the boxcar but as soon as he had that thought he disagreed with it because the boxcar door was wide open.

He knew he couldn't stay rolled up in a ball all the way to wherever he was going. And he knew he couldn't stay almost face down in mud or whatever that was. With the sun rushing the horizon and the train racing from it, Tinkum knew it wouldn't be long before he and whatever was watching him would soon be eye to eye. He had to move. He had to stay. Or he had to jump.

The train ambled on down the tracks. Its sway rocking the boxcar from left to right. The boxcar door rattled and rolled back and forth a few inches at a time. The wind whipped across it like breath across a whistle. Tinkum looked out the opening and could see the front of the train bending back on itself. They were rounding a bend. The force of the turn would soon have him on his back if he didn't soon make a choice. As with everything else in his life, he moved on impulse tipping forward and then in one motion rolling to his right expecting to roll up into a squat and then depending on compulsion leap out of the door or back deeper into the belly of the boxcar.

Rounding up on his haunches, Tinkum lost his balance and bearings when he came face to face with a sulfurous belch and two eyes the color of an algae covered pond. It grabbed him or did he grab it? Locked in each other's clutches, they rolled and wrestled for different reasons. One for his territory. One for his life.

Slips of light darted into the dark boxcar as Tinkum and his counterpart fought. Tinkum kicking and jabbing and avoiding its sharp black teeth. Its callused hands and feet clawing at him. Its growl spewing sulfur. Its hiss spraying spit.

"Out!" It growled through clinched teeth.

"No!" Tinkum shouted.

"Out!" It hissed once more standing over Tinkum ready to pounce again.

It was muscle memory. That was what he told himself. In one fell swoop, Tinkum wrapped his legs around his opponent and like so many times before Indian wrestling with Ram, and Henry and Arvis, he sent the man flying. Flying through the open boxcar door.

By the time Tinkum realized what had happened, the man was nothing more than a divot in a passing hayfield. Easing down into a seated position, leaving his legs to dangle over the edge of the open boxcar door, covered in blood and dung and straw, Tinkum let himself cry.

Chapter Twenty-one

The sound of rushing water and the heat of the afternoon sun roused Tinkum from a sound sleep. His skin itched and his clothes felt too tight. Disoriented and concerned about where he was and what he was waking up to, he didn't move except to look around as best he could without moving his head.

Within minutes he felt the warm rush of comfort flood his bloodstream, he was home. The cave had been his refuge for as long as he could remember and was as much a home to him as the four walls and a roof he shared with Marly and then Bea.

A stabbing pain pierced his left side. Was it from the fight on the train or the thought of Bea? He couldn't tell the difference. Deciding it was neither and more than likely hunger, he pushed away the thoughts of anything but fishing out of his mind.

Leaving his boots on the bank, Tinkum rolled his britches legs up to his knees and waded into the water. The moss covered rocks would have sent anyone else slipping for better footing but Tinkum had walked these rocks for more years than could count. He knew every catfish in the place. Those he had caught and those that remained to be caught. Careful not to stir the water, he worked his way over to a shallow rocky shelf, and bending and reaching into the dark hole under the rock, he pulled out a catfish the size of a kitten and slung him up on the bank. Never satisfied with enough, Tinkum reached in one more time and grabbed another slinging it to the bank to flip and flop and die.

With his meal caught and ready to be fileted, Tinkum made his way back up the bluff and to the cave. Rummaging around until he found his flint rock and the last of a fifth Johnny Walker, Tinkum settled in to his bluff top home and filled his belly.

Sleep had robbed Tinkum of the biggest part of the day. He woke again to the familiarity of the cave. His stomach was once again gnawing at this backbone but he wanted more than catfish and stale drink. Judging by the color of the sky and the moon on his left and the sun on his right, he knew it was well on supper time for everyone below him in Tillman and Fulton.

If he risked going into town, he would soon be met with too many questions and too much judgement. He could make his way to Mud Flats and to Bea but leaving her again would be his or her or both their undoing. And, then there was Fletcher to contend with, and Tinkum had already wrestled one demon in the last twenty-four hours. He didn't have enough gumption to wrestle another.

Thinking on the man on the train sent a cold chill down his back. A chill no amount of comfort could clear his conscious. He had killed him. He was certain of it. If and when the body was found, there would be no way of pinning it on him. No one knew he was on the train. No one knew it was him that threw him off of it. No one but him. He had learned to live with a lot but learning to live with the knowledge that he had killed a man was something he doubted he knew how to do.

Forcing the notion back into the far recesses of his mind to deal with later, Tinkum studied on where to go from here. He could stay on the bluff in the cave for well on a year. He had done it before. Back just after Marly died. He couldn't stand to be in the house. He could hear her laughter at every turn. Hear her call him from around every corner. If it hadn't been for Fletcher Pittman giving him a turn at the plow and a reason to put one foot in front of the other, he would have stayed up on the bluff in the cave and out of that house in the hollow in Mud Flats forever. But, Fletcher saw a need. And, Fletcher had a need. A need to have his field plowed and a husband for his daughter. What Fletcher didn't need and what he didn't bargain for when he fell in with Tinkum Price was a wanderer and two broken hearted daughters.

Tinkum fell back to sleep staving off hunger for a few more hours and the need to decide what his next move would be. Too overwhelmed with the possibilities and responsibilities, he would let sleep sweep it all away.

Hours passed and day turned to night and Tinkum Price worked his way through the woods by instinct and habit. Years spent bouncing around Jessup County's backroads and backwoods made him an expert on getting anywhere he wanted to go without any thought to the route that got him there.

Music and laughter poured from the cinderblock tavern. Neon lights advertising beer brands glowed in the one window sitting high against the front eave. The diamond shaped window in the front door about the size of a man's head flashed and strobed with light from the activity inside. Closer Tinkum could hear the smack of pool balls and someone banging a pinball machine against the wall. He didn't have to be on the inside to know what was going on inside. By the looks of the cars and pickup trucks in the gravel parking lot, he knew just about everyone inside. The screen door rattled as someone or something fell against the front door. Tinkum laughed and rubbed his right shoulder remembering when Arvis had had one too many and Tinkum had teased a bit too long and ended up tossed against the door his right shoulder jamming from the impact. What Tinkum would give right now to see his childhood friends.

Panning the parking lot, he didn't see Ram's truck or Henry's Buick or Arvis's tractor. Not sure of the day of the week, he figured it was a work night for that bunch and two of the three of them were rolled up in bed sheets with their wives. The third one, Arvis, was probably cutting the ceiling boards with his snoring and bad breathe.

Crossing the two lane highway and running alongside the empty lot to the side of the tavern staying out of sight as if anyone within sight could see past the nose on their flushed face, Tinkum made his way around to the back of the building. Hunkered down behind a couple of oil drums used for burning trash and a stack of wooden crates, Tinkum squatted and waited for Red Connors to come out the back door.

"I tol' ya I ain't got need for help. This here's a one man show. Been that way since the beginning. An' like I tol' ya' too, I sure as heck don't need a woman aroun' here." Red pleaded. Tinkum craned his neck to see who Red was talking to but all he could see was the hem of her dress and the curve of her calf. Something inside of him tugged at the corner of his mind because he should have known who she was. The pattern on the dress looked familiar and the way it draped over her calf was familiar too. So familiar that it stirred feelings inside of him. Feelings he had been suppressing for months. Feelings he thought he had killed.

"I know what you told me. And I know you'll keep right on telling me the same thing. I told you, I don't have to be here during regular business hours. I agree. It wouldn't be proper. It's bad enough I'm here right now. But I have to do something. I've got to get to Chattanooga. I've got to find him. Bring him home. She's bad off Red. You just don't know." Olive paused to catch her breath and push down the knot of emotion that was crawling up from deep inside her. "If I don't make me some money. And make it fast. And get down there and get him back here." She paused again. This time allowing her words to sink deep into Red's mind and heart. "Red," She said her voice dropping an octave or two heavy with emotion. "I just hate to think what's going to happen to us both."

Olive waited. Tinkum waited. Red answered, "Alright. Come back later on tonight. After hours. You can sweep up and whatever else that needs to be done. Lord knows I won't complain getting a few hours off my feet. I'll let you work up enough money to get you there and back. But that's it, understand? Nothing more than what you can get done tonight. This ain't going to be an ongoing thing. This ain't a full-time job."

Tinkum slumped against the cinderblock wall. Its cool surface penetrating the back of his cotton shirt. His head was spinning with details. It was obvious to him Olive was talking about him. Somehow she knew he had been in Chattanooga. She sounded desperate. He never heard that in her voice. She was always so sure of herself and every life situation she faced. She was the bravest woman he had ever met. He loved Marly and figured her brave but he hadn't witnessed her bravery firsthand the way he had Olive's. He had watched her stare down Fletcher Pittman over a dustup that would have sent a grown man running with his tail tucked between his legs. He had her stand up to him a time or two also sending a shock through his system he didn't understand or trust. She had a feral streak that ran through her deeper than any wild hair that grew from him. It made him respect her and fear her and love her all at the same time.

But here she was begging. Begging Red Connor's for work. Work she didn't have time for and money she shouldn't need. All for what? To find him. To bring him home. Home to his wife. Suddenly Tinkum's stomach retched causing him to throw up bile. The ache that had been worming its way out of him had made its way through him and he couldn't force it down any longer.

Get out!

He heard the man on the train say. His voice echoing from its dry open grave alongside the train tracks. Fear had sent him running before but he couldn't move. Like the dead man in the hayfield, he was frozen in place.

A cold sweat covered his body. His hands trembled uncontrollably. His feet itched to flee. His ears rang. Rang with the hissing of the dead man's voice. His stomach heaved dry and empty.

"Tinkum? What in the ..." Red Connors said almost stepping on Tinkum as he tossed a brown grocery sack of empty beer cans into one of the burn barrels. "Tinkum! Get up from there. What are you doing hiding back here? Have you lost your mind?" Red hated saying it out loud. It was one thing to have a fleeting thought every now and then that a man like Tinkum Price, having lived through the things that he had and taking to wandering the way he does that sooner or later if not born that way to begin with, would lose his mind. Semple, Red's wife was all the time saying it was a scientific fact that Tinkum couldn't keep living like he was and not face the consequences sooner or later but Red believed there was more to it than science or Semple could explain.

"Red," Tinkum said just above a whisper, "Red. I need." His voice trailed off leaving Red to jump to action instead of conversation.

With a bottle of beer and a handful of pretzels, Red watched as Tinkum sipped slowly on one and chewed deliberately on the other. "You've got a lot of explaining to do. Not to me, understand. No sir. Not to me. But Olive was just here and well, you've got a whole passel of women wondering about your whereabouts."

Tinkum nodded giving time to the beer and the pretzels and his response.

"If you're not careful, you're going to run headlong into one of them here directly. I guess you heard she's on her way back here." Red assuming by the looks of Tinkum that he had been behind the heap of trash the whole time he and Olive were discussing her earning money to go find Tinkum.

Tinkum nodded again testing his stomach and his will to speak.

"I'm not one to give advice but fella I've got to tell ya' I don't want to be within a country mile of Olive Pittman when she lays eyes on you. You understanding me?"

"Yeah," Tinkum said. His breath heavy with the smell of beer and vomit. That handful of pretzels wasn't enough to scrub his palate clean and he needed more than what they offered to settle his stomach. With the dread of dealing with Olive and the long arm of the law reaching out for him soon for killing a man, Tinkum folded forward and emptied his stomach once again of its contents.

"We got to get you out of here and somewhere safe. You're sicker than a dead mule!" Red said turning to go inside. In what felt like minutes, but only because he had blacked out from lack of food and flood of fear, Tinkum was surrounded by voices he knew and trusted.

"Get his leg!"

"I got his leg! You get a leg!"

"Y'all get quite! Can't hear myself think!"

"Watch his head!"

"You watch his head!"

"Ow! Daggumit!"

"I told you be careful!"

"You said watch his head. Not mine!"

"Ignoramus! Didn't figure I needed to tell ya' to watch your own head!"

"You two shut up! Here put him down here. Easy! You're going to drop..."

"Ya' dropped him!"

Tinkum hit the barn floor with a thud and a groan. He trusted Ram and Henry and Arvis. Tonight he trusted them with his life.

"I ain't going to ask you why you've got a bed made up in your barn but I would think if you had one we could have at least got him on it good before we dropped him." Henry said grabbing Tinkum under his arms and lifting again.

Ram grabbed a leg and Arvis grabbed the other both walking towards one another crossing Tinkum's legs and twisting his body pulling his upper body out of Henry's grasp. Again Tinkum's body met the barn wood floor with a thud and a groan.

Henry and Ram and Arvis looked at one another ready to blame the other for the mishap but instead got sidetrack from the expression on their faces and the absurdity of the situation and laughed until they were holding their sides and crossing their own legs.

"Let's just leave him. He looks peaceful." Arvis said catching his breath from laughing.

Ram looked, agreed and tucking his hands under his chin, closing his eyes and snoring sending the other two into a second round of belly laughs.

"Boys, looks like our buddy here has outdone himself this time." Henry said sobering.

Ram sat down on the edge of the bed and wiping tears of laughter from his face studied the unconscious form of his childhood friend on the barn floor.

"Guess it was all going to catch up with him sooner or later. Looks like he has tossed with a bear. Look at those scratches. Got a gash across his eye there. And another across his knuckles. Whatever it was I sure hope it looks worse than he does."

"Y'all remember that time Tink whipped those boys behind the roller rink?" Arvis said stirring up another round of laughter. Henry and Ram both nodded each other staring at their friend on the floor.

"Had all three of them whipped and running for cover before they knew they'd shown up for a fight." Ram said with pride.

"Didn't give us a chance to make a fist. One minute they were there. The next they were hightailing it out. And there he stood, wiping his nose like he got a nose bleed from picking it." Arvis said laughing.

"I know he could get bowed up quicker than anyone I ever saw." Henry added.

"Yeah, 'member that time your daddy said he'd pay double a day's wages for the first'un of us to get that old sow separated in the pen?" Arvis asked.

Henry laughed. "To this day I'm still confounded over how he managed that!"

"That old sow knew crazy when she saw it. She was more afraid of him than he was of her!" Ram said laughing. He kicked Tinkum's boot just as he would if he had been standing reminiscing with them instead of laying out cold on the barn floor.

"Crazy is about right. Reckon Bea is just about gone crazy herself wondering where this one has been all these months. Goldie was over there a day or two ago and said it's just a matter of time before the baby is here. Reckon y'all be heading to the hospital too any day." Henry said waiting for Ram to respond but all he did was nod.

Silence fell around them as they looked at Tinkum on the floor and remembered why he was there and the part they played in it. Each feeling the wait of responsibility once again heavy upon their shoulders because of him, they began to grow restless and needed to escape his presence before guilt and shame and blame took over.

Without parting words, Henry and Ram and Arvis took their leave with Tinkum sound asleep and none the wiser for it.

Chapter Twenty-two

Rain fell in sheets. Steam rose from metal barn roofs. The sun beat through the downpour creating a steam bath. Henry, Ephraim and Arvis waited in the barn. With no sight of Tinkum and the rain falling too hard to go look for him, they decided to pass the time with a hand of cards.

Arvis always on the ready with a deck tucked into the bid pocket of his overalls. Ready to play at the mention of leaving off work, Arvis Ange thought it showed his resourcefulness and not laziness as everyone liked to tease. The few dollars he made and the fistful he generally lost should have been reason enough to leave the cards at home but Arvis was slow when it came to reasoning. Another point of teasing he suffered.

Shuffling Arvis asked what the others were thinking, "Think he's done gone off and got more drink?"

"Barely dried out and back at it is what I'm guessing. You know what they say about a leopard changing his spots. I figure it is just as hard for our ol' buddy Tinkum to change too." Ram said sorting the cards in his hand. Lining up the cards one way then moving them again.

Henry lit a cigar after sorting his hand just the way he wanted it and then turning them facedown. He was more interested in his cigar than the hand he had been dealt. "Wherever he is. Drinking or not. He's got some deciding to do. Goldie said Bea is close to her time. If Tinkum is planning on being here when that baby is born, he better start figuring out how to stay put."

Henry's words were met with a grunt and snort from his friends as they studied their cards.

"I don't think I'd turn down a nice cold drink right about now." Arvis said scratching at the bristle growing on his jaws. "Maybe ol' Tinkum has it all figured out and it's us that need to get in step."

"Arvis you believe that and I've got some bottom land over in the next county I could sell you for cheap." Ram said. Discarding and adjusting the new cards in his hand.

Henry laughed, discarded, taking a long drag on his cigar studying the fire on the end more than the new cards in his hand.

"You say Goldie was over at Bea's? Reckon they've got a plan on what to do when her time comes? I can't see Fletcher being in the middle of it all." Ram paused reflecting on Fletcher Pittman losing his wife in childbirth. "I don't think I could handle it. Not sure Fletch could either. Daughter and grandbaby or not. Has to be hard on a man to go through that again. Fearing it could all come back to roost again." Ram folded. His cards lay lifeless facedown.

"I agree. Can't say I'd be man enough to go through it a second time. Can't say I could handle it the first time. Say what you will about Fletcher Pittman. The man has endured more than the three of us put together." Henry said knowing of the three of them he came closer to truly understanding Fletcher Pittman's state of mind. With Goldie unable to carry a baby to full term, he knew loss. He and Goldie rarely discussed it between the two of them and never mentioned it to their friends and now was not the time to begin changing that fact of life. What was between him and Goldie would stay there. He didn't need to prove anything to Ram and Arvis and Tinkum.

The rain kept falling with no sign of slacking. The heat increased with no draft moving through the open barn doors. The roof was getting a pounding. And the three friends were growing tired of cards and watching and waiting for their prodigal friend.

"Boys, if he don't turn up soon, I'm going to eat these cards." Arvis whined.

Ram snorted, "You ain't going to eat your cards. You might eat this crate here or that tractor tire over there but you ain't going to eat your cards."

Henry joined in the laughing. Everyone knew how Arvis felt about his cards. Kicking at the crate turned upside down as a makeshift card table, Arvis acted as if he was sizing it up to be his next meal sending his friends into belly laughs.

"What y'all carrying on about? Sounds like a party going on in here. I could hear y'all all the way up the road." Tinkum said leaning on the barn door. A half empty whiskey bottle in his hand and his clothes soaked through and through.

"Come on in here and let's deal you in." Arvis said coaxing him inside and way from the downpour.

Henry kicked out milk bucket from against the wall and turned it over giving Tinkum a place at the crate to play a hand. Ram watched with distrust. He, like the other two, knew they were dealing with a drunkard that had something weighing heavy on his mind. Things could get out of hand really fast if they weren't careful.

"Deal me in Arvis. I've got a proposition to make one of you. Might as well let the cards do the deciding." Tinkum said. His aim for the milk bucket was less than skillful and he all but missed it. Henry winced at the pain it had to have caused Tinkum's hip to have caught the edge of the bucket but Tinkum didn't react. The drink had numbed his senses and slowed his reactions.

"Proposition? What's on your mind Tink?" Ram asked ready to get the show going. He was tired and hungry and ready to be done with Tinkum's foolishness.

"Don't rush me there buddy. All in due time." Tinkum said sorting his cards.

Henry understood Ram's impatience. His mind had been on Goldie all day. She had taken on a lot dealing with Beatrix and her sister. He knew Fletcher wouldn't keep away and he knew the twins would fight tooth and nail once the labor started. He was concerned for Goldie's frame of mind and her need to be helpful but the pain it would cause her in the end for being at yet another birthing and being reminded of what she had lost. He loved her so much and would do anything in this life for her. If he could take away the pain and the expectation and the need he would. He knew how it hurt him. To not have a child and to see how it hurt his wife. He was wise enough to know not to assume he would ever be enough. It was a different need. It was a different love. And, it would forever be a difference that separated them from everyone.

The first round went fast. Arvis took what few dollars were laying crumpled in the center of the crate and quickly shoved them deep into his hip pocket. Knowing Tinkum's skill at any game, if he didn't stash the cash fast, it would soon be in Tinkum's pocket instead of his.

Ram still impatient said, "Tinkum, why don't you take your mind off your troubles and lay down over there," Ram nodded to the cot that had been Tinkum's bed overnight, "and getcha some sleep."

Tinkum leaned back against the wall, filled his mouth with whiskey, swallowed hard, and motioned for Arvis to deal.

"Fellows, what I'm about to offer you will change your lives forever. Now, don't dispute me and don't take this opportunity away from me. What I'm offering up to the winner of this here hand is my deed. Nah, nah, settle down fellars. Like I said, don't dispute me. I know what I'm doing. A man lives his whole life expecting to earn a little slice of earth he can build a house and home. A family. A future. A man don't figure in all the things in life that can snatch that dream. That hope. Right out of his hand. Deeds. Fellars, I'm here to tell ya, there ain't no good deed in this life that can erase a bad deed." Tinkum paused to wash his mouth with more whiskey giving Henry time to jump in and try to make sense of his ramblings.

"Deeds? What are you talking about Tink? You wanting to gamble your property because you think you've done something that can't be undone. A bad deed?" Henry asked. His sincere concern cut through the confusion that was mounting.

Ram looked at Arvis and Arvis looked at Ram both realizing without saying it that Henry just explained what they wouldn't have been able to unravel if they worked nonstop for the next three months.

"Yep, that's exactly what I'm saying. Now, pick up your cards boys. Let's play this hand. But, before we get too far, let me make something clear. When the deed goes, everything goes with it. You understand?" Tinkum asked giving Henry a nod to put it into words he can't.

"Everything?" Henry asked for clarity in spite of knowing what Tinkum was saying.

"Everything." Tinkum said.

Ram looked at Arvis. Arvis looked at Ram. They both looked to Henry to explain but he just shook his head in disgust and disappointment. Ram and Arvis too unsure about what was happening played through the hand too fearful to ask any questions.

Chapter Twenty-three

Awave of nausea swept over Beatrix. Retching she leaned her upper body over the side of the bed just missing the bucket of ashes Olive had left on the floor expecting a night of vomiting. She didn't know if it was being a twin that made her in tune with her sister or being her nursemaid for most of her life. Either way, she learned a thing or two about being prepared. What Beatrix did with Olive's preparedness was another matter. At times, there was a sliver of doubt that snaked through Olive's tired mind suggesting Beatrix would do things like miss the ash bucket or forget to cover the slop jar or wad the safety pins up in her bloody rags. Over and over she forgave her sister. Seventy times seven she would mumble as she scrubbed dried vomit from the floor boards, crawled under the bed to retrieve the slop jar lid gathering a layer of dust on her clothes, and dug perfectly good safety pins from the bottom of the washing machine praying one wouldn't get caught up in the motor. The thought of something happening to the washing machine would send her into a rage fearing she'd have to rely on someone like Arvis Ange to fix it. And, that would send her mumbling words of forgiveness all over again. Forgiveness for Beatrix. Forgiveness for Arvis. Forgiveness for herself.

Olive wasn't home to hear Beatrix call out to her. Calling out to tell her she had missed the bucket. Beatrix too sick to care for herself and too selfish to care rolled over and went back to sleep leaving, as she always did, Olive to clean up her mess.

Deep in the woods Olive followed the foot trail that led down to the Red Stagg. Coming to the fork in the trail where many times she went left and climbed her way up to the bluff where she and Tinkum would spend time together, she paused. To her left, a world of memories. Memories that had sustained her until now. To her right, the part-time job that was waiting for her and the constant reminder why she was working. She had to go to Chattanooga. She had to find her brother-in-law. She had to bring him home. Home to his wife. Not home to her.

With one foot on the trail to the right, Olive heard a branch snap and a covey of quail rushed the leafy canopy. Squatting to blend in with the brush, she panned the trail that led up to the bluff from where the sound had come. The moon was high and bright spilling pools of light but not enough to make out distant movement. Whoever or whatever it was it would be right up on her before she knew it had moved again. Her best bet was to stay put and let it pass.

"Best you get up. I see you crouched down over there."

Olive sprang to her feet as if she had sat down in briars. She knew the voice.

"Best you get on over here."

Tinkum recognized the voice and the temper. He wanted to run to her and run from her all at the same time. What he did do and regretted it was laugh.

"Fine with me. Suit yourself. Reckon you just told me all I need to know." Olive said in a huff turning on a dime and marching sure footed toward home.

Still laughing and regretting it Tinkum moved toward her, "Whoa, hold up. Is that how you treat someone you ain't seen in forever?" Reaching for her elbow, he pulled her to him just to have her ball up her fist and plant it squarely on his left jaw sending tears to his eyes, his hand from her elbow and up to his painful jaw, and more laughter from his belly.

"Forever is about right! And, seeing you now makes me wonder just how long forever is. If you ask me, and I don't hear anyone asking me a dang thing, it ain't nearly as long as I'd like it to be." Olive said flexing the fingers on her right and readying it for another fist. Maybe this time to his breadbasket to shut up his nervous laughter. She loved to hear him laugh when something was really funny. But she knew the difference, and he wasn't laughing because something was funny. He was laughing because he was afraid. And, she knew he wasn't afraid of her. If he brought trouble back with him. If he was stupid enough to think she couldn't or wouldn't figure it out. If he was going to sail in only to sail out again. He had another thing coming and it was going to be delivered with her fists.

"I see you've not lost your aim. Your words still cut deep. And," he said still rubbing his jaw, "you're right cross...well, let's just say you've made your point." Tinkum squatted down giving his jaw time to stop hurting. He reached into his mouth and checked his jaw teeth. Nothing was loose. And, then leaning back on his heels, he looked up into Olive's eyes and without saying a word pleaded mercy.

Sadly, Olive wasn't interested in mercy just yet. Still too bent on judgment, she put her hands on her hips and unleashed months of pent up frustration.

"How can you think you can just come traipsing back without a thought to what you've left behind? The mess you caused. Just up and leaving. You know Beatrix. Heck fire, man, you married the woman. Outside of me, you just may be the only other person in this God forsaken world that knows how she is. How can you just up and leave her. Especially at a time like this? How?"

Olive paused but not long enough for Tinkum to speak.

"And, what about me? You just hightail it out of here the minute things get difficult. You tell me one thing one day and then the next you're nowhere to be found. Leaving me to wonder just what you meant by all that you said. Did you mean it? Was it guilt? Don't you think I felt guilty too? She's my sister for God's sakes! Is that what got you? You realized what we had done. What you caused me to do and then I wasn't as pretty to you anymore? Uh, is that how it was? You tell me you love me. You tell me you can't live without me. You tell me it was me! Me! That brought you to our place. And it was me! Me! That got you through all those days and nights Fletcher had you working. But, then I guess when you finally had me. And, the guilt set in on you. You took one look at me and figured if I could betray my sister. Your wife! I could betray anyone! Is that what this is all about! I ain't good enough for you! For Tinkum Price! Is that it?"

Olive paused again. This time to wipe tears from her eyes. Tinkum's heart breaking. He wouldn't speak if he could.

"You know how many days I walked this trail just hoping to run into you like this. You know how many nights I slept in that nasty old wet cave waiting. Waiting for you. You know how many days it has been since I gave up. Gave up on thinking you'd come back. And, just when I get myself thinking straight again. Just when I figured it was over. Beatrix takes a turn and Fletcher sends me to look for you." Waving her hands to tap down Tinkum's sudden need to speak, "Settle down Mister, I didn't come looking for you. I used the money he gave me on Beatrix. Poor thing has needed more than I can provide for her. Been working down at Red's afterhours sweeping the floor and taking out the trash so I could rub two pennies together and make four. You ever stop to ask yourself who was putting food on your wife's table while you've been gone?"

Olive turned her back on Tinkum to collect herself. Her tone had changed and the last thing she wanted right now was to let him off the hook. She had plenty to say to him and she needed a good head of steam to get it all out. Heaven only knows when she would lay eyes on the man again and if she couldn't find answers for her own aching heart at least she'd find some for her sister's.

"Fletcher, I mean, Daddy, thinks I've done been to Chattanooga and back. Don't ask me how he figures I've done it but he does and that's enough to keep him for a while. Goldie helped me with that. Yeah, that's right. You're buddies have been in on all of this too. Tinkum, I'm telling you, you stirred up a real hornets nest this time. Got everyone from Henry and Goldie, to Ram and Milly, to Arvis and Caroline, well when Caroline was living. You know she passed. No, you can't know that because you've been hot footing around. Poor ol' Arvis has all but giving up on living himself. Reckon he's going to be a hermit down in that hollow. Serves him right I guess but that's a conversation for another day. Like I said, Fletcher thinks I've done come and gone from Chattanooga and came back empty handed, of course. I've done more lying for you than I've done for myself and that's saying a lot! You've got me indebted to others too. And, I don't like it. You understand me! I've got my hands full taking care of Beatrix. To have to be reminded every time I lay eyes on Goldie or Arvis that I'm in their debt just about sends me over the edge. It's bad enough I'll be forever and a day asking forgiveness to my Maker for the harm I've brought to my own flesh and blood. But I'll be forever tied to the two of them too."

Exhausted from ranting and the release of emotion, Olive sat down and began to cry.

"Olive? Is it okay if I say something?" Tinkum's voice barely above a whisper and ripe with emotion.

Olive nodded. Her face turned toward her lap. Tears pouring like baptismal waters.

"Let me take you from here."

Olive looked up in shock and confused. She had heard that same statement before. Before he left.

"Come on. Let's get out of here." Tinkum said gently coaxing her to stand and follow him.

It was the same conversation. He had said the same words to her. This must be what people talk about when they say their life passes before their eyes. Her life was passing in front of her like a parade. Same words. Same actions. Same outcome.

Silently, she complied just like before. Linked by joined hands. He leading. Her following. Up the trail to the bluff. Up to the cave. Up to where it all began.

Chapter Twenty-four

The cave welcomed them like an old friend. Tinkum made Olive as comfortable as he could on the makeshift pallet of quilts atop cedar branches. The spicy scent of cedar mixed with the hickory wood smoke masked the dankness. The bluff was pocked with similar spaces. Why Tinkum chose this one Olive never asked but the thought crossed her mind every time she counted off the number of empty caves she passed to get to this one. She tried to remember the stories he told her about the place he came to hang out and sometimes live in but the memories were too fragmented by time and other demands on her mind. In the end, it really didn't matter why. She was here with him. It had become their place to her.

"You're just as beautiful as the first day I saw you. Do you remember?" Tinkum asked. His voice as smooth as the bourbon he was sipping. It reverberated slightly off the earthen cavity.

She remembered. She remembered that day and she remembered every time he has mentioned it since that day. Like it was some red letter holiday on the pages of a keepsake calendar.

"I can't explain it. My heart tore in two and grew two sizes all at the same time." Tinkum paused to swallow the dark amber liquid from the bottle he kept in his boot. He knew better than to offer her a drink.

"In all my born days, I had never seen a woman work a plow and a mule as hard as you worked cutting across that field. Standing there in the road watching, I wanted to save you from your work and save you for myself."

Olive remembered. Her hands instinctively began to ache as she rubbed where calluses now lived where blisters had died. No one would ever compliment her for having soft hands.

"I reckon Daddy helped you get over that real quick." Olive said with a slight giggle.

"You know he did." Tinkum laughed.

Moving over to sit beside her. Sensing the timing was right and she would welcome the gesture and not flinch or react with a fist, Tinkum leaned towards Olive letting their shoulders touch.

"Fletcher knew what he was doing. He saw the way I was looking at you. He knew he had me the minute I saw you." Tinkum's recollections warmed his insides as fast as the Kentucky bourbon he was sipping.

"He saw the way you got all slack jawed with Bea too." Olive reminded him.

Bea was a constant wedge between them. She became his wife as a result of Fletcher Pittman's manipulation and coercion. Tinkum loved Bea the way a boy is taught to love. Soft. Gentle. Tender. But, he loved Olive the way a man learns to love. Desire. Hunger. Ache. He had Bea. She was given. He wanted Olive. She was taken.

"Back then I couldn't tell the two of you apart." Tinkum laughed. He was telling the truth. And Olive knew he was telling the truth. She also knew he was all too familiar with them now to know all the many ways he could distinguish them but she didn't want to spoil the moment by saying something that would sever it. Contrary to popular opinion. She could control her sharp tongue.

Taking another sip from the bottle before returning it to his boot, Tinkum thought long and hard before speaking. Olive felt fear crawl up her back and spread to her armpits. The pulse in her neck pounded at the knot growing in her throat. The soles of her feet itched. And, her scalp pulled tight. Her body was bracing for something. Something she feared her heart wouldn't survive.

Clearing his throat. His way of summonsing strength. Tinkum recounted the last few days as if ticking off a list. "I hadn't said anything to anyone about the man in the car. I had been watching him for weeks. He'd show up for a day or two. Sit out there in his car on the street cross from the house. Just sitting there watching. I knew who he was without asking. Betty was sitting out on the porch. The boy was playing and she was telling me something about Marly and well, I was half listening and have studying on the man in the car. I don't know if she finished with what she had to say or if she got tired of me not listening because the next thing I know she and the boy went inside leaving me sitting there staring at the car and the man inside it. They weren't inside good before he started the motor and drove off.

I came across him later that night. My head was aching to beat the band and I couldn't sleep trying to trace back what Betty had said about Marly. It was the strangest thing. I was all worked up about something I had no idea what but it had my head feeling like it was going to blow up if I didn't get outside. So I slipped out of the house and started walking. I don't know if he saw me leave and decide to follow or what but before I was a good two or three blocks from the house, he was there. Sitting there on the side of the road in his shiny car. Just sitting there smiling like a raccoon caught in lights and the last of your supper in his paws.

I don't know if I said something first or if it was him but before I knew it he was out of the car and on me. He was accusing me of taking something that was his. I didn't know him from Adam but there he was wailing on me landing punches in all the right places. I fought back like any man would to save his life.

Somehow in all the fighting I got my hand on a good size rock. Next thing I know he was laying there in the road. The bloody rock on the street next to his head and me fighting for air.

I'm not proud of it but I took off. I kept walking. Found my way down to the train tracks and hopped a train. All I could think of, my head hurting worse than before, was I had to get gone. I needed to get away from Betty and whatever burden she unloaded on me. I had to get away from the man in the street and his accusations of stealing from him. And, I had to get away from the uncertainty of why I was still there and not here. Here at home where I belong."

Olive turned to rest on one hip and sit where she could see his face better. It pained her to hear what he was saying but she needed to see his face. She needed to know if this was the truth or one of his road stories.

"The train. The train. I've never hopped a train and after what happened I never will again." Tinkum rubbed his face to clear his vision. To see what had happened more clearly.

"Olive. I'm a killer. I left one dead and one dying."

Olive flinched. She didn't mean to but she did. Tinkum saw it and didn't blame her. He would have flinched too. He couldn't blame her if she left right now. Left and called the law and brought him to justice. It was just a matter of time until someone did. If he didn't do it himself.

"The man in the street was still alive. I'm almost certain of it when I walked away. I heard him call out to his wife. I heard him say her name. I don't know if he is still alive. God only knows. But, I do know the man I pushed from the train." Tinkum paused. The words too hard to speak. Lodge inside of him festering.

"The man on the train. He has to be dead. No one could have survived that fall."

Olive sat quietly. She had no words. If she lived to be an old woman she would never be able to repeat what she had just heard. She would never be able to describe the cyclone of emotions spinning out of control inside of her. Olive did what she did best. She refused to believe it. She refused to feel it. She added another layer of stone to the wall she had built around her and refused to let any of Tinkum's troubles inside. She had enough troubles of her own making.

"But that's not the worst of it." Tinkum said reaching out to her only to have her recoil just as he expected. "I can't stay. I've got to get back down there. I've got to turn myself in. I can't let the law catch up with me. If I turn myself in maybe they'll go easy on me. It was all in self-defense. That's what I'm figuring on telling them. It was all in self-defense."

Tinkum got lost in his thoughts and his defense. He didn't notice when Olive got to her feet. He didn't look up to see her stand in the opening of the cave. He didn't hear her say she was leaving. Hear her explain she had to get down to Red's. She had a job. Responsibilities. Bea and the baby.

"I've taken care of everything. You don't have to worry. This time tomorrow or next week or next month, whenever you're ready, go talk to Henry or Ram or Arvis. Or you can catch them all at the same time, it don't rightly matter now. They'll help you. They promised."

When Tinkum finished speaking he looked up at her. The silhouette of moonlight around her body made her look like she just fell from heaven. How he messed things up so fast was beyond his comprehension. How he could ever find his way back was just as far from his thinking. But he had to get back. He had to come back to the ridge. Back to make things right. Back to the life he always wanted. The woman he loved.

Chapter Twenty-five

The nurse fastened the bandage on George's head. She smiled sweetly at Rosalee sleeping in the chair beside the hospital bed. Rosalee was on first name basis with the nursing staff each doing their best to bring healing to George's head wound and Rosalee's fears.

"How you doing today Rosalee?" Peggy the dayshift nurse asked.

Rosalee pushed herself up in the chair stretching her sore stiff back.

"About the same thank you for asking Peg. You think Dr. Baxter will be making rounds today?"

"Not today, hun. It's Saturday. There'll be a different doctor making rounds today. But don't you worry. Everyone is here to get George well enough to send you two home. That's what we all want." Peggy said, straightening the sheet and blanket in spite of it having not moved since George was placed in the bed four days ago. With the exception of the hospital staff, pulling back the covers to check his extremities for proper circulation and nerve damage, and the regular need for the bed pan, the sheet and blanket had been undisturbed.

"Saturday already?" Rosalee said more to herself than anyone else. She was calculating the days and what her son was doing and who was watching him and why Marly had not called on her or sent word. She wasn't so naïve to believe he would actually come to the hospital but at least he could have sent Gus or Betty with word. The only news she got from the boarding house came from a handwritten note tucked inside a basket of cold chicken, biscuits and peach pie left for her at the front desk. It simply said, "Nothing has changed." What on earth was that supposed to mean? Nothing has changed? Everything has changed!

Her husband was in Chattanooga. Found half dead in the middle of the street. Two blocks from the boarding house she had been living in under an assumed name with a stranger posing as her husband for the last several months. How her husband found her changes everything. Now that he found her changes everything.

She had to go back to the boarding house, if for no other reason but to collect her few belongings and to get her son. Nothing has changed would have to wait.

She wanted George to heal but she dreaded it too. He had not said a word since being admitted through the emergency room. She got there minutes after he did. The police brought her to the hospital. She had to ask them to turn off their strobing lights and siren. The look on their faces said it all. The sickening dread weighing heavy on her stomach like a tin roof confirmed it. There was no mistaking it. She didn't want to announce her arrival no sooner than the speed they were taking to get her there. Seasoned police officers, they had seen enough of what regular church going people thought they kept hidden. They didn't need it spelled out for them. She didn't have to have black and blue bruises to prove she was battered. Her countenance was proof enough.

"Ma'am, you don't have to go." The officer in the passenger side said. His partner looking over his shoulder between running red lights to see or hear Rosalee's response.

Rosalee did as she always done. She stayed silent letting others to draw their own conclusions and then acquiesce to their actions.

Not getting a response to not go to the hospital. And since it was regular protocol to transport the next of kin to the hospital, the two officer relied on regulations and muscle memory.

One night spent sleeping in a chair was one too many. Pushing herself up, she paced like a cat at the foot of her husband's hospital bed. He had not woke, had not stirred, had not given any indication at all that he was aware of her being there since she walked into the room. The bandage on his head looked like a lopsided turban. Part of her wanted to laugh thinking of how irritated he would be if he knew how ridiculous he looked in spite of the seriousness of his injury. She always felt small in his presence. His vanity dwarfing hers. If she had any at all. Part of her wanted to cry for him. For her. For their marriage. But looking at him lying there in his sideways gauze hat, his face in a permanent scowl, his hands balled up in fists, she knew she would be wasting tears. It would take more than a bump on the head to bring George Gilford Taggart to his knees in repentance. Something deep within her, reminded her, he was there to claim what was his not beg forgiveness. No, there would be no tears. Not for him.

***

Betty rinsed the last of the breakfast dishes and dried her hands on the cup towel. She had spent the last few days trying to keep things as normal as normal could possibly be at a boarding house. By its own nature, the house was constantly changing but its rhythm had been interrupted. It was the ripple in the current that had Betty on edge. She had come to depend on Rose's schedule. Up early getting young George ready for the day, Rose would fall in to helping in the kitchen and dining room without being asked or instructed on what to do. It was instinctive. Women being territorial, especially in the kitchen, Betty was a good month into the routine before she realized she wasn't threatened by it but enjoyed having another set of hands to help. Now those hands were gone. At least for a little while. She knew the minute her wayward nephew, Tinkum Price, came through the door with a woman and child in tow that she would have to make adjustments. His usual twice a year visit lasted twelve maybe twenty four hours before he got some unseen itch to keep moving. She was forever wishing he would stay put long enough for her to have the conversation she should have had with him years ago but just like the train whistle that blows like clockwork, Tinkum would spring up from wherever he had lighted and announce he was late to some yonder place and off he would go until the next time leaving Betty to long for his return. That was Tinkum's way and she tried to understand it.

With the breakfast dishes dried and put away, Betty weeded the small vegetable garden in the backyard. The morning sun was sliding off the eaves and spilling slowly over the dewy grass.

"There you are. Been looking all through the house." Gus said winded.

"Whatcha need?"

"Nothing. Just wanted to let you know I'm heading out. Got several runs to make today. Might be late 'fore I'm back."

Betty stopped her weeding. Stood up straight. Her hands full of Johnson grass. Her mind full of curiosity. Her son wasn't in the habit of explaining his business. She knew he worked hard and some days were longer than others with the number of deliveries he might have lined up. She never questioned his work and he never explained it.

She stood silent letting him come to the end of whatever was on his mind.

"Just didn't want you to worry." Gus mumbled in the direction of his shifting feet.

What was it about men and their itchy feet? Betty wondered to herself distracted by her son's unusual announcement and uneasy behavior.

Gus didn't get a response from his mother other than silence. Feeling the need to get on with his plans and not prolong the conversation, or lack of it, he raised his hand to wave goodbye then thought better of it and quickly shoved his hand into the pocket of his coveralls.

The morning sun was promising to warm the day quickly and the cab of Gus's panel truck was its first destination. Looking back over his shoulder, he saw the hem of his mother's dress stretched across her freckled calves, her hands busy at work as usual. It was a comfort to him to know she went right back to what she was doing before he interrupted. Before he nearly made an idiot of himself trying to protect her. She was the strongest woman he knew but there were times he wanted to protect her from a world of hurt. This was one of those times.

Betty waited and listened for the grinding gears of the panel truck's engine to warm up and then fade away in the distance. Gus needed to know she was not affected by his behavior. By his announcement. She had spent her whole life protecting those she loved. Her sister, Marly. Her nephew, Tinkum. Her son, Gus. And, now, Rose and George.

As if God heard her heart and responded, a small boy size shadow melted into hers. Resting her hands on her knees she looked up into the fresh face of George.

Chapter Twenty-six

Rosalee stood on the sidewalk in front of Erlanger Hospital playing back the plan like a broken record. She knew she should feel guilty but it had been months since the raw grip of guilt had lost his hold on her. She wanted to feel something. Anything but the numbness. But numbness was all she could feel so instead of fighting it, she gave in to it and let it run its course. It was something Gus had said. Something about letting things run their natural course that gave her the strength to just let go and let things be. What did she have to lose she asked herself. Nothing was the answer. Nothing worth keeping.

The panel truck was heard long before it was seen and Rosalee braced herself for the teeth jarring spine rattling ride up the mountain.

"Been standing there long?" Gus asked leaning across the bench seat and opening the passenger side door.

"Nah, not long at all. Here, got your mama's basket. The chicken and pie was just what I needed." Rosalee forced a smile. Her voice sounded strange and she knew it sounded strange to Gus. They were both nervous. It was obvious. It was expected. It was safer that way. It would keep them from making a mistake of an opportunity.

Trying his best to relax but failing at it miserably, Gus forced himself to keep his eyes on the road and not on Rosalee. She had been at the center of his attention since the moment he saw her at the train station with Tinkum. He gritted his teeth now just like he did that day forced to play along with another of Tinkum's wild schemes. Acting like he didn't know his own flesh and blood. Acting like he didn't know about the boarding house. The very place he had laid his head twice a year since the day he was born.

Gus saw his knuckles turning white from gripping the steer wheel instead of gripping Tinkum's neck. Stretching his fingers to relax his hands and relax his mind wishing away thoughts of Tinkum Price, he pounced on the mention of food.

"Are you hungry? We can stop and get you something. Didn't even think about you not havin' your breakfast yet." Gus pleaded.

Rosalee suddenly felt crowded in the truck cab. His large body seemed to grow larger as his emotions rushed to the surface bloating his appearance. She shook her head and stared out the side window hoping he would be willing to ride in silence for a few miles. At least until they were out of town and climbing the mountain to the cabin.

Like a well-trained dog, Gus read her cues and fell silent. Relieved, he studied the road instead and waited for her next cue.

The logging road was rough. The panel truck rocked from side to side as its tires wobbled over the ruts. The seat springs chirped competing with the axils. The whole commotion stopped as quickly as it started as the road ended at the edge of a lush grassy clearing. Thick shocks of grass sprinkled with wildflowers looked like a lake of green hidden among the towering trees on top of the mountain.

Gus had described it to Rosalee but even with her best efforts she couldn't imagine such beauty. Such stillness teaming with life. Life and light. It was just what she needed. And Gus was right in bringing her here.

"It's just over there. If you stand just here." Gus touched her arm gently and guided her in front of him. "And tilt your head just so." He reached up and placed his hands on both sides of her head, tilting it to the right slightly. "And look there, between those two thickets of Hackberries. See? Can you see it?"

Rosalee was too distracted by the warmth of his massive hands. She expected them to be rough. But they were soft like two huge pillows cradling her head. She nodded but she didn't see anything but a tree line. She didn't know a Hackberry from any other kind of tree. But she couldn't disappoint him. He was trying too hard. And, being too kind.

Suspecting she was just playing along and trusting his eyes better than hers, Gus said, "Well, we don't have to stand here looking. Let's walk on over there. Are you ready?"

Ready? Rosalee thought. Isn't this the whole purpose in driving up here? Chasing away her suddenly disappointment in once again having her expectations too high and resting on a man's shoulders believing he had a masterplan and was easing her through it, she rolled her shoulders back, placed her hand in his and waited for his next move.

Hand in hand Gus and Rosalee cut a trail side by side through the tufted grass. The tree line moving closer and the apron of shadows lifting off the rusted tin roof of the log cabin.

Two whitewashed rocking chairs and water bucket and ladle appeared to be waiting for them on the cabin's front porch.

All traces of dust had been swept away from the rockers and the porch boards. It was obvious Gus had come ahead to clean things up and make ready for her arrival. He had a masterplan. He was just taking his time executing it.

"Won't you have a seat and I'll go fetch some water." Gus said nodding toward the rocker on the right. Without question she sat and watched as he rounded the side of the cabin. She could hear him grunt once or twice and then the sharp scream of metal scratching against itself gave way to the rush of water hitting an empty metal bucket.

Setting the bucket back on the small table between the two rockers, Gus sat in the rocker opposite Rosalee.

"Whatcha think? Is it like I described? I love it up here. Reckon I could live out my days right here on this here porch and not miss a thing or nobody." Gus said sweetly looking out into the curtain of trees they passed through. The green meadow just on the other side. The panel truck standing sentry.

"It's beautiful. Just as you described. But don't you think you'd miss people? I mean as busy as you are running from here to there always being around folks. Talking and visiting and doing business. Don't you think you'd miss it? Miss someone?" Rosalee wasn't sure if she was talking about Gus or herself by the time she stopped rattling.

Gus just shook his head no as if he had already worked through that problem and came out on the other side long ago.

He had built the cabin for a time such as this. A time to sit on its porch with the woman he loved. The woman he wanted to grow old with. The woman he wanted to weep for him over his grave. He wanted that woman to be Rosalee.

"I'm sorry. I shouldn't have said that." Rosalee smiled wishing she could take back her words miss reading the pain on his face.

"A man can live his whole life and miss what's right in front of him." his voice fell an octave or two as he spoke to the space between his feet. Rosalee turned her body slightly giving her full attention to his words.

"I reckon I've been that man. I've done what I was told since the day I took my first breath. Followed the rules. Walked the line. And what's it got me? But all that changed the day I saw you. My life ain't been the same."

Finding courage in the head of steam that had been building inside of him, Gus knelt down in front of Rosalee, took her hand between his and declared his undying love.

"Rosalee, I know you're not free. And, I'm not asking you to break the law. Man's law or God's law. I can wait. Wait until you are free. Free to be mine. All mine. I know what I can offer can't compete with the life you had in Nashville. But, what I have I give to you freely. I give you my heart. Do with it what you will."

Tears ran down Rosalee's face. Her heart felt like it could explode. She never knew a man's love until this moment.

Chapter Twenty-seven

The full moon filled the woods with light and shadows. Unable to sleep, Olive walked without reservation or hindrance over damp limestone and gnarled roots. Weaving in and out of pine thickets so thick she could get lost if she didn't know the landscape like the back of her hand. Turn left at the burned out stump. The one lightning hit leaving it a mile marker for her and Tinkum and anyone else that passed over the ridge through the woods to the bluff. Turn right and keep right and watch every step through the gap and eventually you come out in Tillman. Olive rarely went that way when it was easier to take the road to Tillman. Tillman was never an interest to her. No one she cared two hoots about lived there and anything she needed or wanted could be found just as easy on the square in Fulton.

She lost count the number of times she passed through the woods to meet Tinkum up on the bluff. She long since quit counting. The number no longer meant anything. Anything but pain. Pain she couldn't afford to nurse.

She walked the familiar path humming a sad song. Hours earlier she had been listening to the radio. The pop and sizzle over the airwaves broken by the Carter Family. The mournful voice of another woman singing the words locked in Olive's heart.

"I never will marry or be no man's wife
I expect to live single all the days of my life..."

Climbing the earthen staircase. Limestone jutting out from the steep side of the ridge placed there by an unseen hand. Olive stopped at the top. Her hands on her hips. Catching her breath. The sorrowful lyrics swimming in her mind.

Hearing the river roar just ahead and needing to see and feel its power, she walked with purpose to the bluff's edge. Memories sliced through her mind. Flashes of light like lightning in a thunderstorm. Tinkum sitting beside her. The gentle curl of his smile. The sparkle in his eyes. Eyes dancing with mischief and longing and secrets.

The tree tops behind her caught a high flowing breeze. The leaves applauded. An owl asked who and her heart answered him. Her skin reacted to memory and the breeze. She rubbed her hands up and down her bare arms and regretted she didn't grab the blanket off the bed before leaving the house.

The sudden thought of the house sent her mind back to the empty bed she just left. The radio, her secret keeper, spilling tonic and poison all at the same time and the words of the song echoing.

The house where Beatrix lay swollen with new life. Tinkum's baby. Olive's fingernails cut deep into her palms but she didn't feel the pain. Not from her palms or from her knuckles as she pounded the rocky shelf where she sat overlooking the river below. Hot, salty tears fell from her eyes closed tight soaking her cotton gown. She wiped away the tears. Smearing blood.

The heartrending pain ran through her like the river's channel. It was gone as quickly as it came leaving behind a calmness just as unsettling. The song continued to echo in her mind. Playing out like a script of her life.

She spoke the words of the song to the dark waters below. Her shoulders sank. Her chest fell. The trees stood silent. And the river patiently waited.

Again, the tears welled and spilled. Clutching the jagged edge of the rocky bluff. Feeling the achy release and the coolness of the stone against the searing half-moons pierced into her palms, Olive leaned forward and screamed "Tinkum!" into the black waters.

Her heart gave way to her mind. The fight was over. Never again would she feel his touch upon her skin. Never again would she feel his warm breath whisper into her ear. Never again would she wake beside him as he watched her sleep.

Rocking back and forth on the ledge. Giving way to the years of waiting. Watching. Wanting. Letting it all go from her. Making room. Room for another. One that would love her unconditionally. One that would never leave her. One that would call her mama.

Olive waited once more. Waited until everything she had carried inside her emptied into the water below never to surface again. Waited with reverence and when she was all hollowed out she sealed the hole in her heart.

***

Beatrix woke to a wet bed and an unbearable pressure forcing her to push. Her parched throat could hardly make sound but still she screamed for her sister. Days on end she wondered what this moment would be like but nothing she imagined compared to what she was experiencing. And, nothing prepared her for her reaction to the sudden pain and the one person she needed. Her sister.

The preacher had been by to visit just yesterday. And it was just yesterday that he said the oddest thing. Meant to be a comfort but had become a burr in her brain, he said it was in pain that we face the truth. Beatrix didn't know what truth she was facing in this pain but she did know the only person worth facing it with was Olive.

Grabbing the bedsheets, she pulled herself up to a seated position to find relief but the minute she did she regretted it. Falling back she screamed again but silence answered.

Crying hysterically and begging God to intervene, Beatrix believed, like her mother, she would not live to see her newborn baby. She had spent her whole life letting first one and then another make her believe she was just like her mother. Too frail. Too small. Too pitiful. Only she knew her strength. It was there. Waiting. It took all the strength she had to not say something about the way people talked about her. Didn't that count? Whoever it was in this world keeping score, didn't it count that she never fought back. Never showed disrespect. Never stood in judgement over the ones standing in judgement over her. If anyone was paying attention, they had to know it took enormous strength to see and keep silent.

The first rays of dawn flooded the room with its pink glow. Beatrix's sweat covered body rippled with involuntary movement. With or without assistance, Beatrix's or anyone else's, the baby was coming. He would be here before the sun was fully dressed for the day.

Out of desperation, Beatrix called out for her sister one last time. Olive heard her name just as her bare foot met the first porch step. Clearing the porch and most of the threshold, she was at her sister's bedside before the next labor pain hit.

"Trixie! I'm here. Trixie! I'm here now!" Olive cried. Holding her sister's trembling hand and wiping sweat soaked hair from her face, she wanted to crawl up in the bed and do this for her. Not out of pride or jealousy or arrogance but out of love. She called her Trixie. There had only been twice, maybe three times in their lives when Olive called her twin sister Trixie. It was a term of endearment born out of a deep abiding love. Patient. Kind. Protective.

Leaving Beatrix's side for two seconds, Olive called Milly Hatch. Later she would regret it but for now Milly was her only hope of getting this baby born and keeping her sister alive.

Della answered the phone. "Ha-looo?"

Gritting her teeth to keep from cursing at the child, Olive steadied her voice and politely asked to speak to her mother.

"Ma-ma!" Della's tiny voice trailed away from the receiver. And what felt like days but was only seconds, was a faint conversation between mother and child about answering the telephone. Milly's voice grew louder the closer she got to the receiver.

"Ah, hello? Who's calling please?"

"Milly, come quick. The baby!" Olive dropped the phone missing the cradle leaving Milly to hear Beatrix moaning in the background.

Leaving Della in charge of her younger sisters and grinning like a bored housecat, Milly pulled her apron from the kitchen hook and fumbled with the sash as she made her way across the field between the two houses as fast as her swollen feet could carry her. Each step sinking deep into the soft dirt. With her baby due any day, she couldn't afford rushing her own labor.

The screen door slammed behind her. She didn't care and the sisters didn't notice.

"Have you checked her?" Milly asked at the foot of the bed.

"No. Thought I'd leave that to someone that knows what they're doing." Olive said making a point not to mention she just got here herself.

"Alright then, Bea, let's take a look." Milly turned her full attention to Beatrix.

Olive didn't mind being pushed out of the situation. Because outside of the situation is where she had been for a long time. She also didn't mind that Milly didn't ask the obvious. Because Olive had grown tired of lying to herself and everyone else about Tinkum. It felt good for a change not to have his name mentioned. It felt real good.

"Olive, crawl up there behind her and help her push." Milly gave orders with precision and politeness. Olive had no idea what she was being asked to do but she did as she was told and hoped for the best.

Sitting behind her sister, Beatrix leaning against her, Olive leaned forward giving ballast to her sister's pushing. Her posture reminded her of sitting on the rocky bluff. Her mind wandered to just moments earlier when she placed her love for Tinkum in its watery grave. Without realizing it, she began humming the tune.

"Now that's pretty. Listen to the song Bea. Don't fret." Milly encouraged.

Olive felt a pang of guilt but kept humming fearing Milly's reproach and Beatrix's labor.

"One more good push and..."

Olive wrapped her arms around the small slope of her sister's waist. Beatrix's damp arms draped limp and lifeless over her sister's. Olive leaned and hummed. Beatrix winced and pushed.

"It's a boy! You've got a fine little man here!"

Olive's humming gave way to the baby's crying.

Chapter Twenty-eight

"**W**hat no kiss?" Tinkum teased.

"Nope." Olive said without apology. "I didn't come to kiss you."

Tinkum laughed but they both knew there was no humor to what was said.

Standing where they had met so many times over the years. The place had a different look now. It was dull. Lifeless. It made Olive's skin crawl for more reasons than she knew. Tinkum thought it was just because he hadn't been there in a while. That it had somehow lost its luster to him. Just one more reason for regretting being gone too long.

"Place don't feel the same." Tinkum admitted.

Olive looked around but said nothing. The river roared below the bluff. Had it been four months since she buried her love? No the place didn't look the same to her either.

"I reckon we can fix that. Been way too long." Tinkum reached out to take her hand.

Olive stood still. Tinkum's hand hung suspended between them.

"Ain't it something how we just know when the other one is near? I mean who else in the world do you have that kind of connection with? I can tell you I ain't got it with no one."
Tinkum couldn't tell if he was confessing or seducing. Her coldness was throwing him off and he was so tired of lying that he dreaded the sound of his own voice.

"Why don't you just shut up? I'm here for one reason and one reason only. You know as well as I do that Red told me you were back in town. He told me you'd be up here expecting word about the baby. Figure even a snake knows when to crawl out from under his rock. So that's why I'm here. The baby."

Olive held out her hand. Closed fisted. And as if she was offering him a snake, Tinkum drew his hand back quickly.

Reaching for his hand, she gave him a woman's handkerchief. Its folds concealing two small bundles. Peeling back the white cotton fabric, Tinkum's hand trembled when he saw the pink ribbon tied around a strawberry blonde lock of hair and the blue ribbon tied around a small blonde lock of hair.

"They're gone. Neither suffered. You're free now. Free to roam this world till you run out of places to go. No one here to keep. Not no more." Olive's words fell like stones landing hard and heavy at his feet.

Tinkum stared at the locks of hair. One his wife's. One his son's. The river roared or was it the sound in his ears. He didn't know. He wasn't expecting any of this. Red never let on there was any trouble. His friend of twenty years. A man he thought of as an older brother. A man that knew more about him than he knew of himself never said a word.

The woman he loved. The one he shared secrets and made plans. The one he trusted. Standing cold as a pillar of salt. Speaking as though she is talking about the weather and not her own flesh and blood.   His mind couldn't reconcile what he was hearing. His heart couldn't hold that much pain.

Olive misunderstood or didn't care about his reaction. Either way, she turned to go just as he grabbed her and pulled her to him.

"Don't leave. Not now. Can't you see? I love you. I'm nothing without you. I'm nothing."

Olive waited until he let go. She smoothed her hair back in place. Pulled her shoulders back. And, trusting her feet would not fail her, turned and walked away. She kept walking hearing him call out her name. Before she reached the rocky steps, he no longer was calling out to her. Curiosity almost got the best of her but she refused to look back believing he was standing there watching and waiting for her to do just as he expected.

Weak kneed but full of resolve, Olive eased her way down the steep rocky outcropping, holding on to the side of the ridge and grabbing saplings along the way to steady her descent. Once at the bottom, she walked the few miles down the ridge to the hollow with the bend in the road and her girlhood home.

"Got y' errand ran?" Fletcher asked spewing tobacco spittle into the grass. He had been whittling when she left and by the looks of the stick he had been working on, he was no closer to finish than when he started.

"Yes sir. They still sleeping?" Olive asked taking a seat on the porch swing. Something Beatrix was fond of doing.

"Hadn't heard a peep from 'ire one of 'em since you let out."

"That's good. Good for them to rest. She'll feel better for it and he'll grow stronger."

"That's what they say."

Silence settled between them except for the soft snoring from inside the house.

"Ye hear that?" Fletcher asked grinning. His few teeth black with tobacco and rot.

"I hear it." Olive smiled too.

"Well, I best get back at it. You planning on staying close?"

"I'll be right here. Got nowhere else I need to be."

Pulling up tall. Stretching out his lower back. Fletcher looked out over the field waiting for his attention and the plow. "I'll be back directly."

"Alright. Reckon those two will sleep awhile longer. I'm going to wait until I hear them stir before going inside. We'll eat a cold supper if that sits with you."

"Sits fine. Just fine."

The gentle creak of the porch swing chain kept any thought of Tinkum from entering Olive's mind. There would be time enough to let guilt or shame or regret creep in but for now what was done was done and it was done for good.

***

Tinkum stood on the edge of the bluff looking out where the rocks jut out down the slope. His knees and lower back ached from standing still for too long but he feared if he moved, if he gave up, she wouldn't come back. She always came back. No matter how many times he disappointed her. No matter how many times he lied. No matter what, she always came back.

How could she leave him now? Now in his distress. In his loss. She was all that was left. Didn't she know how much she meant to him? Didn't she know it was her that kept him coming back to a place filled with more loss than hope for him? She was is refuge. A hope he had depended on since the day he saw her behind that plow.

He had made a deal with Fletcher Pittman. Work for his daughter's hand in marriage. Fletcher's intentions were to find a future for Beatrix. Tinkum's intentions were to make a future with Olive.

He got wise to Fletcher's intentions and refusing to let the man holding all the cards get the better of him, Tinkum decided to take it all. Take the one being offered. And, take the one he wanted.

Standing in the place that had been their hiding place. He now hid what was left of the two that deserved more than he could offer. Kneeling down and digging a hole with his bare hands, he placed the handkerchief with its precious gifts tucked inside into the hole and covered it over.

Taking the bottle from his boot, he drank until he feel asleep. Night fell around him and morning burned into midday before he woke beside the small place where the earth had been turned over. Patting it down and wishing he knew how to pray, Tinkum Price once again found the courage to walk away.

Chapter Twenty-nine

Rose paced the cabin's wood floor. The silence bore down on her. She missed the noise of the dry cleaners. It had been days since she was there and she feared Eunice would assume she was not returning. She feared it herself.

Back and forth she paced. Wringing her hands. The silence deafening. Her mind racing to keep up with the flood of thoughts. It was in the cabin's silence she realized that was what made home unbearable.

It wasn't Gilford's absence. It was the massive silence that filled the space when he was no longer there. A wake on a still body of water. She knew she could fill her days with activity. Busyness for the sake of busyness. George was enough to keep her busy. It wasn't for the lack of things to do that plagued her. It was the aching emptiness that was left when Gilford was not there.

Standing in the middle of the mountain cabin, she knew what she wanted. It took the space between Chattanooga and Nashville, between a mountain cabin and the dry cleaners, and between no husband and pretend husband. It took these last several months. It took almost a year. It took her time to see all she needed was within her own grasp. It has been there all along. It was in her own making. She knew if she kept waiting for someone else for her happiness she would never find it. But, she knew also she didn't have to be alone to be happy.

Determined more than ever before, Rose made up her mind to resolve things with Gilford. Collect George. And, go home.

Gus bounced along the logging road making mental notes to bring the box blade up the mountain with him tomorrow to spend time working the washboard ruts out of the packed chirp. Plans. His brain was spinning with plans.

A late fall wedding spread out in his mind's eye. He could see it. Folding chairs from the church sitting side by side across the front yard of the cabin. The fall color on the mountain as the backdrop. His bride, Rose, dressed in a dress of her own choosing. He would see to it. She would choose exactly what she wanted and not worry about the cost or wishing for something more. Days of wishing would be over. Over for Rose. Over for him.

His mind's eye trailed across the people sitting in the folding chairs. George in his first pair of long britches. A suit of blue with a thin pin stripe. His shoes shining. His hair oiled back. Gus imagined the broad smile on his mother's face. The lace handkerchief she used to dab away tears from the outside corners of her eyes. His mind traveled over every happy face. Every person he knew, he imagined, would travel up the logging road to the clearing, to the cabin, to witness the happiest day of his life. The day he takes Rose as his wife.

He could imagine everyone with bright smiles except for his cousin Tinkum. Try as he might, his mind could not force a genuine show of happiness across Tinkum's face. A dark cloud crept up the mountain. It circled like crow. And, finding its home, it settled in the back corner of the congregant and perched on the shoulder of Tinkum Price.

Gus pushed the truck into low gear and tried to push the bad thought out of his mind. He didn't want to be thinking of Tinkum when he got to the top of the knob. He didn't want Tinkum intruding on his time with Rose. He didn't want Tinkum to come between him and the plans he had in place.

Hearing the truck engine. The first recognizable sound she had heard all day. Rose smoothed her hair back and forced a smile to her face. She stepped out onto the porch and waited to see the massive figure of Gus parting the tall grass with his tree stump legs.

Waving to her as if she could possibly miss seeing him coming across the meadow, Gus looked too eager. Too happy to see her. She couldn't match his enthusiasm and it made her sick to her stomach. She dreaded what would come next. She had no idea what she would say but she knew something had to be said.

Living like this was just not for her. His pledge was tender and she knew he would be hurt. It was unavoidable. But, she had already spent too much of her life trying to keep everyone around her happy at the expense of her own happiness. Why everyone can't be happy with no one missing out was beyond her comprehension but she was willing to figure out how it could be done. If she realized anything spending time in the silence of the cabin and listening for the first time what her heart had been trying to tell her, she wasn't responsible for anyone's happiness but her own.

"How ye doin'?" Gus said several strides from the porch.

Rose just kept smiling and waiting. Acting like she didn't hear him or was too lady-like to shout a response. As if anyone, or anything on the mountain gave two hoots about being ladylike.

"I didn't think I was ever going to get here." Gus said panting.

Concerned something happened in town. Rose braced herself for the worse. Was it Gilford? Had she waited too long before coming to the realization that it wasn't his fault for her unhappiness? If she had waited too long she wasn't sure she could forgive herself for being so selfish.

Was it George? Had something happened to George? She had left him too long in the hands of those that enjoyed his company but could not care for him like his mother. If anything happened to her son. Her baby. She could never forgive herself.

Anger rising up her spine. Rose knew she spoke too harshly but she had to know.

"What's happened?"

The look on Gus' face said it all. She had jumped to conclusions. The silence had raked across her nerves leaving her raw and exposed. She couldn't handle the slightest suggestion of anything out of the ordinary. She couldn't tell the difference between casual conversation and serious concern.

"Rose, Honey, I'm sorry. I shouldn't have left you here alone. I see that now. I thought I should have brought George up here but I just needed. No, wanted. Guess it's time to be honest. I wanted time alone with you. There will be enough time for everyone else. I wanted time to let you know how much I care for you. Rose, please sit down. There's nothing wrong. Everyone and everything is fine. I've been all day trying to make my way back here to you. To tell you once and for all that I love you and I want you to be mine."

Rose hung her head. She didn't care what Gus thought of her reaction. Her emotions were stinging her insides like a hive of bees. Hours ago Gus left saying he had an errand to run and would be right back. It was that moment. The way he just left her there with no thought to how she felt about being left that made her realize why she left Nashville.

Pacing back and forth she worked out what had been stewing in her mind for months. She had left Nashville because for the last six years she had watched as Gilford left her every week with no thought to what he was leaving behind. She gave in to the loneliness like a comfort but it was cold comfort.

When Gus rambled down the mountain with no apparent thought to leaving her in an unfamiliar house. With no thought to what she would do with the day. With no thought to when he would be returning. She knew then, she knew she wouldn't stand by and let another man leave her and take her for granted again.

She had spent the last several months finding her courage in the noisiness of the dry cleaners. She found it too in the deafening silence of the cabin. She knew she was strong. It was time to let everyone else know just how strong.

"Take me back." Her voice broke with emotion.

"Back?" Gus sounded more confused than he was. His brain and heart trying desperately to keep up. Trying desperately to manage the moment. Turn it back to his favor.

"Yes. Back. Take me back. Back down this mountain. Back to the hospital. But, first stop at the boarding house. I want to get George."

Gus interrupted. "But, George is too young to be at the hospital. They won't let him…"

Rose looked up. The determination in her eyes pierced his heart. He swallowed hard and didn't say another word.

Not speaking but understanding each other completely, Rose and Gus walked slowly back across the meadow. They each got into the panel truck. Gus behind the steering wheel. Busying himself with starting the truck. Rose on the passenger side. Staring out the window trying hard to force herself not to remember the beauty of the mountain. She would think back on this day years later and she didn't want to regret leaving the mountain.

Chapter Thirty

It's always darkest before the dawn. That's how the saying goes. Gus listened to the words roll around in his head. They sounded like the clanking of mason jars. Mason jars filled with corn liquor. The sound he had grown so accustom to winding around mountain tops and dipping down into the deepest hollows that he didn't hear it any longer. The words took the place of the clanking glass. Around and around he drove. Up Grays Point. Down Gooseneck Rim. The yellow headlights cutting through the early autumn fog separating the filament for the truck to pass through.

His mind was just as foggy. No sleep and sampling the supply made a bad situation worse. Gus couldn't remember a time before Rose and he couldn't remember a time before yesterday when he felt this heart sick.

How could he go from being on top of the world to wanting to crawl in a hole and die in one day? Common sense urged him to pay attention to the road in spite of the fact he had been running these roads since he was tall enough to touch the brake and see over the dashboard. Common sense demanded he put her out of his mind in spite of the gaping hole in his heart he knew he would never fill with anything like her again. Common sense pressed in on him warm, comforting and strong like a loyal dog. A big dog.

The truck lurched forward. Its brakes wet with condensation. The yellow headlights created a wall of light ten maybe fifteen feet between the truck and a stand of pine trees. The still was another twenty yards ahead through the woods along the creek. Killing the engine and the lights, Gus trusted his memory and his feet to make his way to the still.

Gus heard Turtle's cussing before he saw the fire and smelled the smoke.

"Ye going burn the woods down!" Gus laughed.

"Ah, don't you ever mind. I know what I'm doin'" Turtle said spitting and cussing and tapping out his burning britches leg.

Still laughing Gus came closer to inspect the damage and assess whether he would be rushing out of the hollow and back to town with Turtle. Back to the hospital. The same hospital where Rose's husband lay waiting for his wife. For his family to be reunited.

Gus didn't know if it was being at the still, its sweetness sinking into his belly or if it was being with Turtle and his never ending foolishness. Whatever it was that made the fleeting thought of Rose less painful was worth its trouble because if he could have a moment's peace from missing her, he believed he could learn to make a habit of it.

"Take a seat and tell me something." Turtle said turning his attention to Gus and away from his singed britches and leg hairs.

Gus settled down on a stump, scratched his bristled chin and searched his thoughts for something to share.

"Got everything delivered. That little'un of Dupree's is a corker!"

"Ruby?"

"That's the one."

Turtle laughed expecting a good story.

"Got over there just after midnight I reckon. Fog had done settled in so all I could make out was Dupree and one of his kin. I'm guessing his nephew. Least ways that's who it looked like. I'd seen him a time a two before. I bit taller now. And a bit ganglier. But, that face. You know all them Duprees look alike. Put one in a crowd of a hundred and you going to know which one is a Dupree every time."

"It's the nose."

"Yep. I reckon that's what it is. Hooked like buzzard."

"They's all buzzard nosed."

"Well, old man Dupree and his nephew was just standing waiting like always out by the fence row when I pulled up. I rolled down the winder and commenced to passing one jar after another. They took five by the way this time. Just so you know. Said they'd be settling on five going forward."

"Five you say?"

"Five."

"Well, so I reckon I got the last one out the winder and was just about to pull off when out jumped that little'un right smack dab in the middle of the road and she was as naked as a jaybird! Had her thumbs in her ears wagging her hands and sticking out her tongue!"

Turtle choked laughing. Asking, "Naked?"

"Son, you ain't seen two men move so fast and juggle moonshine at the same time! Old man Dupree passed his load of jars to the boy and grabbed that little'un up just a kicking and a screaming. He had her by the waist. Her head pointing south and her rump pointing north. You ain't heard the likes coming out a little'un's mouth! It was enough to shame the devil!"

Gus took a long sip from the jar resting against the stump. The clear liquid burned his throat and warmed his insides. Wiping his mouth with the backside of his hand he finished his story between belches.

"There I sat. My truck burning gas for no good reason. Me staring at the boy. Him staring at me. And old man Dupree warming the backside of that little'un all the way back to the house. He was hollering orders for her to hush up and for the boy to stop his gaping and get the shine in the barn."

Gus passed the jar to Turtle. Turtle took a swig. Wiped his mouth and passed it back. Nodding for Gus to go on with his story.

"There she was wearing nothing but her imagination and old man Dupree was lighting her up for sassing. Don't that beat all?"

Turtle nodded. "I reckon he's got his hands full over there with a whole passel of buzzard nosed kin. He's probably figuring it's going to be hard enough marrying her off. If'n she takes to running around naked you'd hope she'd at least have a sweet disposition."

Gus laughed then turned melancholy.

"Sweet disposition ain't enough sometimes."

"Ye talking about your Rose?"

"She ain't mine. Not no more. Probably never was."

"What ye talking about? You took her up to the cabin didn't ye? You tol' her ye loved her didn't ye? You tol' her yer plans didn't ye? And she what? Refused ye?"

"Yep. You got it buddy. She refused me"

Standing to check the still and tend the fire, Turtle gave Gus time with his thoughts. He didn't need any more details than what was shared. If Gus wanted to offer more it was up to him. Friends don't stay friends for long by prying.

"She's going back. Back to Nashville. Reckon she's packed and ready to go by now. If she ain't by his side." Looking down at his pocket watch and then returning it to its pocket. "I probably should have left well enough alone. Trying to turn a woman that late in life. Trying to convince her to start over like some young thing that ain't never shared a marriage bed. Never took vows. It was better left unsaid. I wasn't ever going to win her. No amount of persuasion. No amount of affection. No amount of anything I could say or do was going to change the way things turned out. I've got to know that or I'll go on thinking about her. Wanting her. Loving..."

"Well there's always Ruby Dupree." Turtle said with a chuckle

Gus bent double laughing. The innocent expression on his friend's face and the sincerity in his voice ended his self-pity. Gus knew where he belonged.

Chapter Thirty-one

Sleet fell outside while Bea rocked the baby inside by the wood burning stove. The sweet smell of hickory smoke soothed her. The baby had cried all night from colic. Nothing she or Olive or Fletcher could do could ease his misery. They tried everything. Catnip tea. No relief. Warm bath. No relief. Belly rub. No relief. Exhaustion brought sleep for the baby, Olive and Fletcher.

In the stillness of the house, the sleet bouncing off the tin roof, Bea found herself wishing she was back in her own home. She was more than grateful for Olive bringing her back to Fletcher's. Despite feeling lost in the home she had known since the day she was born. Born in the room she now rocked her own baby. She appreciated all her sister and father were doing for her and her baby but she had a husband out there and if she wasn't at home, their home, when he came home, he may think she gave up and left him.

The thought of her doing the leaving felt as foreign as being a married woman with a baby living in her father's house with her sister providing for her. For her and her baby. Bea had to get back to Mud Flats. But first she had to do the hard part. She had to tell Olive and Fletcher.

"Coffee?" Fletcher asked walking through the room scratching his rump. The hair on the sides of his hair slicked straight up from tossing and turning. His eyelids swollen from lack of sleep and trying too hard to stay asleep.

"Sounds good." Bea whispered. Eyeing Fletcher and then the baby. Fletcher winced. Looked down at the little bundle wrapped in his mother's arms and a quilt. Sure he had not woke him, he forced a weak smile at his daughter and returned to making his way to kitchen to make coffee. Distracted by the sleet falling outside Fletcher stopped to surmise the weather and make mental plans of what the day's chores would be for him and for Olive. Leaving Bea to care for the baby and to regain her health, Fletcher and Olive had worked the farm just as they had since the twins were old enough to do a day's work.

"Gonna be a mess out there today. Ollie still sleepin'?" Fletcher asked still looking out the window. Not waiting for Bea to answer. He answered, "Yeah, best let her get plenty of sleep now while she can. I'll get the coffee on and get to the barn. If she gets up. Send her own. If not. Let her sleep. She'll be riled but we can handle it." Fletcher laughed at his own joke. Bea understood his meaning. Smiled and closed her eyes to catch a few more minutes of silence.

The smell of coffee mixed with the hickory sweetness. Bea pulled it in deep. Inhaling and exhaling slowly and deliberately. She appreciated Fletcher's kindness and the ease in which he entered the day. It wouldn't last long. It never did. But those few moments in the beginning when his guard is down and the day is new, he was tolerable. Manageable.

"Little man finally doze off? Bless his heart. Wore himself out. How you doin' this mornin'? You get any sleep?" Olive asked warming her backside at the woodstove. Fully dressed and damp from the sleet. She had already been out to the barn. Took care of the cows. And was back inside before Fletcher knew anything had been done and was back inside.

"Fletcher..." Bea whispered.

Olive looked out the window towards the barn.

"He'll find something to do while he is out there. Always something to do. But don't you know he'll never say anything about me getting there before him. He'd come nearer swallowing his tongue before he admits he needs me."

"If you only knew the kindness he showed you just this morning."

Bea regretted it before she got it completely out of her mouth. Bracing herself for the retaliation. Hoping when it came Olive would remember the baby and not raise her voice above a whisper. She knew she could do it. She had hiss better than most Cottonmouths on the ridge. And she carried just as much poison.

"Never you mind what Fletcher says or doesn't say about anything around here. If he's wasting his time with any sort of kindnesses he is doing just that wasting his time."

"Olive, when are you going to stop that talk and see how he cares for you. For both of us. Look at what he has done all these years. Look at what he has done just these last months. Taking care of us. Seeing we had a roof over our heads. Food to eat. Clothes on our backs. I can't think of a time we needed for anything. He didn't have to do it. He could have turned tail and..."

Beatrice stopped just short of comparing her father and her husband but what stopped her was the look on Olive's face. The words struck a nerve. Bea had painted a picture. She had carried Olive back through time and rubbed her nose in her every moment she blamed Fletcher for every wrong that had ever been done to her as if it had been at the hand of Fletcher. Tears filled Olive's eyes and Bea regretted summonsing them.

"We're more alike than you realize Bea."

"What's that supposed to mean? Of course were alike. We're twins. Couldn't be more alike if we were the same person. If we were one."

"Just remember, Sister, just remember, you said it. Not me."

Olive wrapped her coat around her and walked outside. She stopped for a few seconds on the porch. Wiped the sleet from her face. Or was it tears? And stepped off the porch and around the house.

Bea rocked. Patting the baby and hummed. Not for him but for her. Silence filled the house again. Out across the yard glazed in frozen rain, Bea watched Olive's car pass by.

"Everything's fed and warm. Time we do the same. Let me get my hands washed and I'll get some biscuits in the oven." Fletcher said puttering around the kitchen like a housewife. Fat and sassy and satisfied to have his daughters home and his grandson under his roof, Fletcher Pittman was ready to tie on an apron and take up needlepoint.

Bea eased up standing and stopped to gauge if the baby was going to stay asleep. Sure he had not been disturbed by her movement she took one step, waited, and then took another making her way to the kitchen. She smiled big and wanted to laugh but thought better of it seeing her father meander around the kitchen. Sifting flour, pouring milk, scooping lard, folding, kneading, cutting biscuits, he slid the baking pan into the hot oven and turned his attention to the cast iron skillet warming. Flour, grease, salt, pepper, fork scraping, slow pour of milk, fork back and forth, back and forth, gravy thickening.

"Grab us a plate, cup and the butter. Give that little man a taste of this here gravy. That'll set everything right." Fletcher laughed at his own joke.

Beatrice prepared her breakfast plate with one hand and found pride in herself that she could do it so naturally. Filling her mouth with biscuits and gravy and coffee. She filled her head with ways to break the news to Fletcher that she wanted to go home. Her home.

"Looks like you got something on your mind. Best spit it out. Your insides are going to get tied up as tight as his."

"You always could see right through me."

"You never was one to put on airs. It's what separates you from the rest of the world. There's virtue in being honest Beatrice. Virtue."

Beatrice didn't feel virtuous. She had to get home. She knew it wasn't going to be long before someone got news to Tinkum wherever he was that he had a son. And, she knew she struck a nerve with Olive. She knew if she didn't get home and be there when Tinkum found his way back and have his son there waiting on him that when he did come back he would be coming back to Olive.

A virtuous woman didn't hold secrets. And she had gotten good at keeping the biggest secret she had ever had. She knew about Olive and Tinkum. She knew they were in love. She would have to be deaf, blind and dumb to not know what was going on right in front of her. Olive isn't as cunning as she thinks she is and Tinkum isn't as clever as he thinks he is. And, she isn't as innocent as everyone thinks she is.

Pushing her plate out from her, Beatrice pulled her baby closer to her and cleared her throat. "I've got to get home."

Waiting to let the words settle. Waiting to let Fletcher come to terms with them.

"You are home."

"No. Daddy. My home. I need to get home."

It was the way she said it that made the difference. In a few words, everything came full circle for Fletcher. He had tried to ignore the obvious but now it was out in the open or at least as out in the open as it was going to get. He knew, or at least he thought he knew, because he knew what could happen with two women and one man, under one roof. He had watched the three of them for years. He knew Tinkum had feelings for both of them. And he knew but had not, could not, would not, admit he had played any part in the threesome.

Pushing his plate out from in front him. Wrapping his hands around his coffee cup. Studying the coffee. Avoiding eye contact. Fletcher resolved to not stand in her way.

Beatrice waited for Fletcher to make an excuse to leave the table before she packed hers and the baby's things to go home.

Chapter Thirty-two

Sleet gave way to snow. Flakes the size of goose feathers tumbled from overcast skies landing quietly on ice. The farmer's almanac would later record it as the largest snow fall in Jessup County history. For Olive it was just one more thing to get under her skin. She hated the snow. Hated everything about being cold. About being shut up indoors. She would never admit it. Not even to herself. But she understood in some small way, how Tinkum could take to the roads. If she knew she would make it out of the hollow without freezing to death, she would let out and not turn back.

Bea had been laid up in the bed since she brought the baby back from Fletcher's. Overestimating her strength and ability to care for herself, let alone anyone else, she was sick within two days of being home sending her right back to bed and right back to Olive nursing her back to health.

The hollowness Olive had come to accept inside herself was quickly being filled with resentment. An old familiar friend, resentment fueled her every thought and action. If it wasn't for the striking resemblance to Tinkum, she would resent the baby too.

"Olive? The baby. Is he dry? Have you fed him?" Bea's weak orders raked over Olive's skin like sandpaper.

Olive did her best to ignore her sister but the more she pleaded and questioned the more she wanted to smother her with the bed pillows. Olive's brain was hot with foolishness and she had long since quit tapping down thoughts of how to end her suffering and Bea's all at the same time.

By the time anyone found Bea's dead body, Olive was certain she would have an alibi even the preacher would believe.

Days spilled into weeks. The snow laid around waiting for the sun. And, when the sun came it brought rain. Again, the farmer's almanac would later record the historic flooding.

"Bye oh baby – bye oh bye" Olive sang rocking the baby to sleep. The drone of her alto voice soothed him to sleep and eased her frayed nerves. Her resentment had turned a corner and had grown into resolve. She had a plan. She wasn't certain how she would execute it but at least she had a sense of direction. Something she hadn't felt since the day on the bluff in the early morning hours when she tossed her love for Tinkum into the Cumberland River and later held his son in her arms.

With the baby fast asleep, she placed him beside his mother. Fever had held Bea captive for over a week. Olive wasn't certain how much life was left in her sister. It was the least she could do for Bea. To let her son lay next to her if these were her final minutes left on this earth.

For over week, Bea only stirred now and again and when she did it was with crazy fever talk. Nonsense about dogs fighting over a bone. She had just about sent Olive running out into the storm during the night when she sat bolt right up in bed screaming at what only she could see. Olive braced herself against intervening knowing the fever would spike and send her sister back into the quiet darkness of sleep. Between the thunder and lightning, the hammering of the rain on the tin roof and his mother's feverish screaming, it was a wonder the baby slept at all.

Olive woke to the sound of banging just outside the bedroom window. Half a wake and half asleep it took her several minutes to realize she had been dreaming. Hearing the banging in her sleep. She had been dreaming the sound was Tinkum stomping snow from his boots standing just inside the front door. The door wide open and the rain pouring like sheets behind him yet he was covered in snow. Looking like something the cat dragged in, he didn't speak a word in the dream but as she played back the images in her mind she knew he had come back for her. Passing the bed where his wife lay lifeless, he made his way to Olive. In the dream, she hands the baby wrapped in white to Tinkum but instead of the baby Tinkum holds a folded handkerchief in the palms of his hands.

The banging continued demanding Olive's attention. The bed frame rattled with each blow from the side of the house. Olive held her breath and listened. The rain sounded like a sledgehammer on the roof. And, whatever was slamming itself against the outside wall would soon be on the inside.

Fearing the worse but knowing she couldn't stay put, Olive forced herself out of the bed and looked out the bedroom window. Tractor tires filled the glass as flood waters shoved the massive contraption against the house. The water had overturned the tractor sending it racing down the hollow and deposited it for now against the house. How long it could stay there without becoming dislodged or worse, coming through the wall, was anyone's guess.

Lightning cracked like a bullwhip sending Olive racing around for her clothes. Checking on the baby and Bea, she left them where the lay sleeping as she made her way to the front door. The front door that had held the dream of Tinkum coming home to her.

The rain had swelled overnight to a roaring flood. Trees the size of man sailed passed in the rushing current. A set of tricycle handlebars and tailgate floated by like echoes of lost time. Olive stood with her toes curled over the threshold leaning out as far as her arms would stretch trying to see up the hollow but the pouring rain and fear pushed her back.

A snake slithered by undisturbed by the pounding rain. The current swift and strong pulled at the rickety porch separating it from the house. In the time it took Olive to piece together what was happening, the muddy water ripped the porch off its braces almost sending her tumbling out the open door.

Everything was happening too fast for Olive to keep up. Time spent milling about the small house was ending right before her eyes and she wasn't ready. She wanted to undo every bad deed. Every misspoken word. Every evil thought. But time was up. She had set her course long ago and whether she was up for the challenge or not it was playing itself out. Right here. Right now.

Tinkum. If only Tinkum would come back. If only he would step up this one last time. Come stomping through the front door just as she had dreamed he would and take her. Her and the baby.

Looking out the door one last time hoping against all she knew to be true, she looked one more time for Tinkum to come over the hill at the top of the hollow making his way home. Instead, what she saw was Ram and Arvis in a boat. Waving their arms. Motioning for her to come on out. Join them.

Turning to get the baby, Olive pulled the bedspread from off Bea, wrapped it around her and the baby and returned to the front door.

"Don't this beat all?" Arvis asked as if he was somehow taken by surprise at the flood.

"Easy now. Take it easy." Ram said steading the boat right up against the house where the porch had been.

Olive stepped into the boat refusing anyone's help. Holding the baby against her chest, she braced herself against the rain and the rising water and her rescuers.

Before Arvis or Ram had the chance to ask about Bea, the muddy water poured through the house pushing them out into the current to witness the destruction.

***

Olive tied the white ribbon under the baby's chin. The bonnet fit just as she had hoped. The white christening gown would serve double duty at his mother's funeral.

Everyone stood around in their Sunday best as the preacher recited the Twenty-third Psalm. Thud after thud rose from the grave as soft ground packed well for the grave diggers. Voices signing Amazing Grace tried to drown out the sound of the grave filling and the occasional sob but nothing could drown out the mournful wailing of Fletcher Pittman. He had known too much loss and every heart within earshot was breaking right along with his. Every heart except for Olive's.

Standing by the graveside, watching as the shovels tapped out the last remaining air and flowers were placed over the exposed earth, she hugged the baby to her and breathed in his sweetness. He was hers. Tinkum's son was hers. While she had been hatching plans of her own. Tinkum had been making plans too. In a hand of cards, he had given everything away. His home. His son. His future. And, he bound the winner to a lifetime of obligation. Arvis and Ram and Henry explained it all and Olive was determined to hold them to their obligation. Not knowing who held the winning hand, she held them each responsible.

Everyone said their goodbyes and slowly made their way up the gravel road and to the church for fellowship and fried chicken. Everyone except Olive. She knew he would come. And she wanted him to see her. See her standing there with the baby. See everything he could have had but gambled away.

She couldn't see him. It was a shadow in the shape of a man on top of the hill in the shade of the tree line. But her heart told her it was him.

The End

From the author...

Strength comes in many forms. For me it has mostly been in the form of the women in my life. My grandmothers were the strongest women I've known. I was blessed to have known them both for most of my life – losing them both after I too had become a grandmother.

They taught by example. Living their lives in an unapologetic fashion they taught me to trust in God and in myself. It is with gratitude I say thank you to Alma Lee Rogers and Addie Maxine Brown for giving me the resolve to weather the storms of life and for teaching me how to be comfortable in my own skin.

I was blessed in life to have known my great-grandmothers. They too had a unique strength that has gone matchless throughout my life. Tennessee Olivia Eden, Eddie Wilma Briley, and Brittie Dale Brown taught me the mysterious beauty of perserverance and I will forever be grateful.

These women gave life. My aunts, cousins and my mother each possess an imprint of their mothers. Each shaping me and giving me inspiration for the stories write.

The Deed is dedicated to these women.